THE HE

Tania then turned to Rupert feeling tearful.

"You really cannot leave me like this. I *must* say goodbye to you."

Rupert did not reply and as she climbed out of the carriage, the front door was opened by the night footman.

Rupert turned to his coachman,

"Wait for me, Wilkins, I will not be long."

The coachman raised his hand to his hat and Rupert walked into the house beside Tania.

There were only a few lights left on in the hall and they made for the drawing room.

For a second Tania was afraid that her stepmother's guests had not left and she would be still there.

They went into the drawing room and then Rupert closed the door.

They were in complete darkness with the exception of the moonlight coming in through one window where the curtain must have been left undrawn by mistake.

It was letting in a silver light that touched the floor.

For a moment they stood close to each other.

Then slowly, as if he had no wish to frighten her, or to spoil the magic that was enveloping them both, Rupert drew Tania close into his arms.

"I love you, Tania" he breathed. "Try to remember me, and, as you said, pray for me every day. I will dream of you every single night I am away – "

THE BARBARA CARTLAND PINK COLLECTION

Titles in this series

1. The Cross Of Love
2. Love In The Highlands
3. Love Finds The Way
4. The Castle Of Love
5. Love Is Triumphant
6. Stars In The Sky
7. The Ship Of Love
8. A Dangerous Disguise
9. Love Became Theirs
10. Love Drives In
11. Sailing To Love
12. The Star Of Love
13. Music Is The Soul Of Love
14. Love In The East
15. Theirs To Eternity
16. A Paradise On Earth
17. Love Wins In Berlin
18. In Search Of Love
19. Love Rescues Rosanna
20. A Heart In Heaven
21. The House Of Happiness
22. Royalty Defeated By Love
23. The White Witch
24. They Sought Love
25. Love Is The Reason For Living
26. They Found Their Way To Heaven
27. Learning To Love
28. Journey To Happiness
29. A Kiss In The Desert
30. The Heart Of Love
31. The Richness Of Love
32. For Ever And Ever
33. An Unexpected Love
34. Saved By An Angel
35. Touching The Stars
36. Seeking Love
37. Journey To Love
38. The Importance Of Love
39. Love By The Lake
40. A Dream Come True
41. The King Without A Heart
42. The Waters Of Love
43. Danger To The Duke
44. A Perfect Way To Heaven
45. Follow Your Heart
46. In Hiding
47. Rivals For Love
48. A Kiss From The Heart
49. Lovers In London
50. This Way To Heaven
51. A Princess Prays
52. Mine For Ever
53. The Earl's Revenge
54. Love At The Tower
55. Ruled By Love
56. Love Came From Heaven
57. Love And Apollo
58. The Keys Of Love
59. A Castle Of Dreams
60. A Battle Of Brains
61. A Change Of Hearts
62. It Is Love
63. The Triumph Of Love
64. Wanted – A Royal Wife
65. A Kiss Of Love
66. To Heaven With Love
67. Pray For Love
68. The Marquis Is Trapped
69. Hide And Seek For Love
70. Hiding From Love
71. A Teacher Of Love
72. Money Or Love
73. The Revelation Is Love
74. The Tree Of Love
75. The Magnificent Marquis
76. The Castle
77. The Gates Of Paradise
78. A Lucky Star
79. A Heaven On Earth
80. The Healing Hand

THE HEALING HAND

BARBARA CARTLAND

.com

Barbaracartland.com Ltd

First published on the internet in May 2011
by Barbaracartland.com

ISBN 978-1-906950-59-0

Printed and bound in Great Britain by Cle-Print Ltd.
of St Ives, Cambridgeshire.

THE BARBARA CARTLAND PINK COLLECTION

Barbara Cartland was the most prolific bestselling author in the history of the world. She was frequently in the Guinness Book of Records for writing more books in a year than any other living author. In fact her most amazing literary feat was when her publishers asked for more Barbara Cartland romances, she doubled her output from 10 books a year to over 20 books a year, when she was 77.

She went on writing continuously at this rate for 20 years and wrote her last book at the age of 97, thus completing 400 books between the ages of 77 and 97.

Her publishers finally could not keep up with this phenomenal output, so at her death she left 160 unpublished manuscripts, something again that no other author has ever achieved.

Now the exciting news is that these 160 original unpublished Barbara Cartland books are already being published and by Barbaracartland.com exclusively on the internet, as the international web is the best possible way of reaching so many Barbara Cartland readers around the world.

The 160 books are published monthly and will be numbered in sequence.

The series is called the Pink Collection as a tribute to Barbara Cartland whose favourite colour was pink and it became very much her trademark over the years.

The Barbara Cartland Pink Collection is published only on the internet. Log on to www.barbaracartland.com to find out how you can purchase the books monthly as they are published, and take out a subscription that will ensure that all subsequent editions are delivered to you by mail order to your home.

NEW

Barbaracartland.com is proud to announce the publication of ten new Audio Books for the first time as CDs. They are favourite Barbara Cartland stories read by well-known actors and actresses and each story extends to 4 or 5 CDs. The Audio Books are as follows:

The Patient Bridegroom	The Passion and the Flower
A Challenge of Hearts	Little White Doves of Love
A Train to Love	The Prince and the Pekinese
The Unbroken Dream	A King in Love
The Cruel Count	A Sign of Love

More Audio Books will be published in the future and the above titles can be purchased by logging on to the website www.barbaracartland.com or please write to the address below.

If you do not have access to a computer, you can write for information about the Barbara Cartland Pink Collection and the Barbara Cartland Audio Books to the following address:

Barbara Cartland.com Ltd., Camfield Place,
Hatfield, Hertfordshire AL9 6JE, United Kingdom.

Telephone: +44 (0)1707 642629
Fax: +44 (0)1707 663041

THE LATE DAME BARBARA CARTLAND

Barbara Cartland who sadly died in May 2000 at the age of nearly 99 was the world's most famous romantic novelist who wrote 723 books in her lifetime with worldwide sales of over 1 billion copies and her books were translated into 36 different languages.

As well as romantic novels, she wrote historical biographies, 6 autobiographies, theatrical plays, books of advice on life, love, vitamins and cookery. She also found time to be a political speaker and television and radio personality.

She wrote her first book at the age of 21 and this was called *Jigsaw*. It became an immediate bestseller and sold 100,000 copies in hardback and was translated into 6 different languages. She wrote continuously throughout her life, writing bestsellers for an astonishing 76 years. Her books have always been immensely popular in the United States, where in 1976 her current books were at numbers 1 & 2 in the B. Dalton bestsellers list, a feat never achieved before or since by any author.

Barbara Cartland became a legend in her own lifetime and will be best remembered for her wonderful romantic novels, so loved by her millions of readers throughout the world.

Her books will always be treasured for their moral message, her pure and innocent heroines, her good looking and dashing heroes and above all her belief that the power of love is more important than anything else in everyone's life.

"I have always believed in the power of prayer and there is no doubt that Florence Nightingale's phenomenal ability to heal the wounded came from her prayers and belief in God."

Barbara Cartland

CHAPTER ONE
1854

Tania gazed dreamily out of the window of the train as it flashed past and thought just how attractive the French fields looked.

The hard working men and women in them seemed to have a romantic atmosphere about them.

It was something she did not see in England.

She was thrilled to be travelling in one of the new fast trains which ran from the *Gare du Nord* to Boulogne.

It was the first time she had been in one and it was even more exciting than she had expected.

Tania had been at a school in Paris for the last two years.

She knew she would never forgive her stepmother for not allowing her to come home so that she could have said goodbye to her beloved father before he died.

Her stepmother, however, had been adamant saying that she must stay at the school in Paris until her education was completed.

She fully realised it was not because Lady Amesly was interested in what she learnt.

In fact she had known from the moment her father had remarried after her mother's death that the new Lady Amesly had found her a nuisance.

And she certainly did not wish to chaperone Tania into the Social world.

Tania recognised that life was going to be difficult.

The first thing she must do when she arrived back was to pick up the threads with her friends and relatives.

'I expect, as we are living in London, it will not be too difficult,' she tried to reassure herself.

At the same time she could just hear her stepmother saying in the voice she always used to her stepdaughter but never to her husband,

"You will stay away in France, Tania, until I decide when you can return."

It became even more complicated when she turned eighteen which was last May.

Her stepmother had written to the Mother Superior of the school, which was part of a French Convent, to say that Tania was to stay there as long as possible.

She was indeed prepared to spend more money on her education, but it was money her stepmother obviously begrudged her.

After Christmas the Mother Superior sent for Tania and spoke to her very kindly,

"We love having you here at the school, Tania, and you have been an exemplary pupil, but you are older than the other girls and I think you should now go back to your home. I sincerely hope you will eventually find someone you love and be married."

Tania had not wished to leave.

But she knew in her heart that the Mother Superior was right in thinking that she was too old to stay on at the Convent School.

It was a most exclusive school that accepted only the daughters of Noblemen or Royalty, whether they were English, French or any other nationality.

It was now the beginning of February and she was being sent home despite the protests of Lady Amesly.

"I would have kept you another month, dear child," the Mother Superior had said, "but it so happens that Sister Agnes is going to London for family reasons, and this is a good opportunity for you to travel with her."

She was well aware that the Mother Superior was always annoyed when the nuns had to be taken away from teaching to escort some girl who had to return home during the term time for whatever reason.

There had been one pupil last term who had to be escorted home as far as Egypt and the history lessons had suffered.

Sister Agnes taught English and the school would have to find a temporary tutor until she was able to return.

Sister Agnes was most upset at having to go back to England to be with a dying relative and she had come away from the school in a distraught state of mind.

Tania spent several hours on leaving Paris trying to soothe Sister Agnes.

"I know he will die before I can get home," she was wailing.

There was nothing Tania could possibly say except that she was sure – which she was not – that Sister Agnes would arrive home in time.

She had often wondered why religious people made such a fuss about death – if they believed that someone was swept up into a perfect Heaven, why should they weep so much for those who had passed on?

She suspected that it was they themselves who were frightened of death.

Her mother had taught her to pray when she was a child and she had always believed in some Power overhead directing her life and taking care of her.

She had no wish to return home now after her dear father's death.

Her stepmother disliked her and she knew that she would not be a welcome member of the household.

She prayed that God would support and help her, and that somehow things would work out for the best.

The train was moving at what she considered was a tremendous pace and she continued to gaze out at the view sweeping past the window.

Sister Agnes appeared to be sleeping – at any rate she was silent in the seat at the far end of the carriage.

They fortunately had the carriage to themselves as the Station Master himself had locked them in before they left Paris, promising them that they would be much safer and more comfortable alone.

They were due to reach Boulogne early tomorrow morning where there would be a ferry waiting to take them to London Bridge.

The Mother Superior had informed Lady Amesly of the time of her stepdaughter's arrival.

Tania was hoping that a carriage would be waiting for her and that would mean she could give Sister Agnes a lift to wherever she had to go.

Suddenly she heard the brakes screech and the train rapidly slowing down.

Then there was a violent thump.

It was so violent that Tania was instantly thrown roughly onto the floor.

As Sister Agnes screamed out hysterically, the train came to a standstill with a great many bumps and lurches.

It took Tania a moment or so to realise that there had been a crash.

She picked herself up from the floor and sat back on the seat she had just been thrown off.

Sister Agnes was lying stiffly where she had fallen and was now whimpering rather than crying.

"I am afraid there has been an accident," Tania said somewhat unnecessarily.

There was no answer from Sister Agnes, but there was a thunderous noise of voices shouting outside.

The door of the carriage was unlocked and a man in uniform put his head in to ask in French,

"Is anyone injured?"

"I don't think so," Tania replied in French.

"Everyone has to get out so we can clear the line."

"What on earth has happened? What have we hit?" demanded Tania.

But already the man had moved away to the next carriage.

Slowly, because she felt somewhat unsteady, Tania rose to her feet and pulled Sister Agnes up onto the seat.

"You are not hurt," she insisted, seeing no blood, "and we have to climb out now."

"I am far too ill. The shock has killed me," sobbed Sister Agnes weakly.

Tania thought it would be useless to argue with her, so she went to the carriage door to see if there was anyone who could help.

There were several women rushing around outside screaming or in floods of tears, whilst the men were trying to pull their possessions out of the carriages.

Looking up the line Tania could see that their train had crashed into another one travelling slowly in the same direction and fortunately it was a goods train.

Tania thought that a lot of the women were making an unnecessary fuss – they were being overly hysterical, not because they had been hurt, but simply because there had been an accident.

She could see no one at the moment who she could possibly ask to help Sister Agnes.

And she could hardly jump out of the carriage and leave her alone.

Then she could see walking down the line towards her a tall good-looking young man she felt instinctively must be English.

As he reached Tania's carriage, he started to say in French,

"Are you all right? Is there anything I can do?"

"Oh, please help me," Tania implored him. "There is a woman here, a nun, who thinks she is injured, although I suspect she is just upset at being thrown onto the floor."

The Englishman – she had been right in thinking he was English – smiled at her.

"*You* don't seem to have been damaged."

"It certainly was a shock," Tania answered, "and I can see now that we have run into the back of another train in front of us!"

"Sheer carelessness on the part of those running the line," he responded. "But mercifully our driver saw it far enough ahead to be able to apply his brakes in time to avert a disaster. They say that once the line is clear there will be another train to take us on to Boulogne."

"Well, that's a blessing anyway, but what shall I do about Sister Agnes?"

"I should imagine she is your chaperone and should be looking after you," the Englishman commented, but he was smiling as he spoke.

It was clearly a statement and not a rebuke.

He climbed into the carriage and persuaded Sister Agnes to lie full-length on the seat.

"I don't think she is injured," he said in a low voice to Tania.

"I am sure she is not. We both fell forward at the same time and, although a shock, it has not hurt me at all."

She looked anxiously at Sister Agnes, whose eyes were tightly shut and so were her lips.

"I will see if I can find something for her to drink," offered the Englishman.

"That's a good idea. I am sure that what she would really like is a cup of tea."

The Englishman laughed.

"That is very English, but as we are now in France, I think it will have to be something more stimulating."

"You must *not* give her alcohol. She is a nun and they are not allowed to drink."

"Then I am afraid it will have to be water. There is a restaurant car at the front of the train."

Tania had been told this before she left Paris, but it meant they would have to get out and leave their luggage unattended in their compartment.

The Englishman had already clambered out of the carriage and he now held up his hand, obviously intending Tania to accompany him.

She thought it would be rude if she did not do so.

The nun, although she seemed almost unconscious, would guard their luggage.

She therefore jumped down.

As the Englishman took hold of her hand, he pulled her through the crowd and then they walked up to the front of the train.

Next to the engine, as the Englishman had told her, was the restaurant car.

Tania could see that mercifully the crash had been much less severe than it might have been.

But when they looked in through the windows and the door they saw that the impact had smashed the tables in the restaurant car and everything was broken.

There were pieces of china and broken milk bottles everywhere and a huge pot of coffee must have fallen near the entrance.

"We cannot go in there," exclaimed Tania.

"I could try," the Englishman suggested doubtfully. "But I think it would annoy the engineers who have just arrived to move the trains off the lines."

"Is there no hope of our being able to travel on our train?" Tania asked him.

"I think it most unlikely and it may take a long time to clear the lines, in which case I should imagine they will send another train for those who are going to Boulogne."

"Do you think we will have to stay the night here?"

"It looks rather like it, but I am certainly hoping we will not. My carriage is full, so there will be no question of being able to lie down to sleep."

"It may not be as bad as we expect. Try to find out from someone how they are coping with the collision."

The Englishman looked round.

She felt he had a strong personality like her father, who always got what he wanted and people obeyed him.

A moment later she realised what the Englishman was looking out for.

A small engine drawing one small car came down the line and stopped behind the goods train.

Out of it stepped a railway official wearing a much more important looking uniform than those on the train.

He was, she recognised, someone in authority.

The Englishman walked up to him.

"I am so delighted to see you, monsieur," he said in very good French. "I hope you will be able to tell us how soon it will be before we can continue our journey."

"You must give me a chance to look at what has happened, monsieur," he replied. "But I think we can get you safely to Boulogne in good time to catch the ferry that is taking you to England."

The Englishman smiled.

"If that happens, I commend you for your services," he said. "It is important for me to be in London as soon as possible."

"If you will please give me your name, monsieur," the Frenchman enquired.

"I am Captain the Honourable Rupert More, son of the Earl of Grantmore. You must understand that I am on my way to join my Regiment. I think many Frenchmen are doing the same."

"I suspect, monsieur, that you are referring to the war that is likely to break out against Russia."

"I see you are well informed," he answered. "And although I hope it is untrue, we have been told that France and England are now both committed to defending Turkey against Russian aggression."

Tania could see that the Frenchman was delighted that an Englishman should know so much.

"You are quite right, monsieur, and it is something we must prevent, although none of us is anxious for war at this moment."

"I agree with you," replied Captain More. "But the Russians are getting too big for their boots and it is time we did something about it!"

The Frenchman laughed.

"Well, of course, under the circumstances you must certainly join your Regiment as quickly as possible. Is this lady with you?"

Captain More turned at once to look at Tania.

He understood from the pleading expression in her eyes that she did not want to stay behind with the train.

"I'll tell you what I will do for you, monsieur," the Frenchman suggested. "You can travel down to the Station ahead in the car I have just arrived in. I believe there is a train there which will carry a few of these passengers on to Boulogne. The rest will have to wait until we have cleared the line."

"That is exceedingly kind of you, monsieur, and I am most grateful."

"Then go collect your luggage and don't mention to anyone what you are doing, otherwise I will be bombarded by others and I usually travel in that small car alone."

"I understand and thank you again, monsieur."

He turned round to take Tania by the hand.

"Let's go and collect your luggage," he suggested, "and I hope there is not too much of it."

"I am wondering," Tania sighed, as they moved out of earshot of the French official, "what we should do about Sister Agnes."

"She will join us later," the Captain replied firmly. "The French will surely not want to accommodate and feed a great number of people unnecessarily. I am quite certain that your nun will catch up with us later on, perhaps after midnight."

Tania was thinking it would be wrong for her to take such an advantage and leave Sister Agnes unattended.

When she returned to the carriage, she found to her surprise that Sister Agnes was not alone.

Another nun from a different Order was sitting by Sister Agnes and was now smoothing her forehead gently with a handkerchief and talking to her softly.

She was kneeling down by the side of Sister Agnes, but she rose when Tania entered the compartment.

"How kind of you to help Sister Agnes," she began. "She has had a great shock and it has upset her badly."

"I can see that," the nun, who was French, replied, and I will, of course, tend to her. I don't think she is badly hurt."

"I don't think she is hurt at all, but she did not feel very well when we joined the train."

"I will look after her," the new nun promised.

"That is very kind of you and I am very grateful. I went to fetch something for her to drink, but unfortunately the restaurant car has been badly smashed up and nothing seems to be left intact."

"I have some milk in my own compartment."

"And we have some sandwiches."

"That is splendid! I expect you have come to move your luggage so that you can transfer it to the train which is coming to rescue us."

"That will take a little time, so please do tell Sister Agnes not to worry about me when she comes round. We will meet up with each other on the ferry."

"Yes, of course I will tell her," the new nun replied.

While Tania had been talking to her, Captain More had been removing the luggage from the overhead rack and was placing it outside.

"That is not all mine," Tania told him.

"All the luggage has to be taken out of the train," he said, "and it will be placed on the other one which is yet to arrive. All bags stowed in the Guard's van will come automatically to the ferry. And I would suggest, as we do not want to lose the special privilege we have been offered, that we hurry up and take our place in the official's car."

"I am sure that you are right. I would hate to miss reaching the ferry as quickly as possible."

"I agree with you it would be very stupid – "

So the Captain then picked up Tania's suitcase and her dressing case which were not particularly heavy.

Without saying anything more they walked up past the other train to where the car was waiting.

Captain More put Tania's luggage inside, then went back to fetch his own.

He was back very quickly with a suitcase and what appeared to be a gun.

Then, as he placed the cases safely in the car, he pointed out,

"In case you are worried, my shotgun is not loaded and I brought it with me because I expected to go shooting with a friend on his estate near Paris."

"Were you not able to join the shoot?"

Captain More shook his head.

"I was, as it so happened, otherwise engaged."

He helped her onto a seat inside the car.

Then without saying anything more, he went back the way he had come.

She wondered if he had gone to tell his friends, if he was travelling with any, what was happening or perhaps he had merely gone to retrieve more luggage.

She realised, however, there was room for three or four other people in the car and she only hoped that his seat would not be taken before he reappeared.

Tania need not have been perturbed as he returned alone.

A moment later the driver stepped into his seat and started the car's engine.

Captain More sat beside Tania and to her delight it moved off without anyone else coming with them.

"I thought that we might have attracted some other passengers," she whispered to him, so that the driver could not hear.

It was not likely he would have understood if he did because she was speaking in English.

"I was afraid of the same thing," replied Captain More. "But the French official, who is obviously of some importance on the Railways, must have considered that you and I were more distinguished than those other passengers.

"Therefore we've been given the Royal treatment of travelling to the ferry and making ourselves comfortable there before the hoi polloi arrive!"

The way he said it was so funny that Tania laughed.

"I think we are behaving rather badly, but this is so much more comfortable than sitting about until it's dark."

"And," added Captain More, "perhaps with nothing to eat and little to drink!"

Tania laughed again.

"You have been so clever and thank you very much for including me."

"How could I possibly leave you behind when you are so beautiful? You might have had a most unpleasant time with some offensive stranger."

"I was supposed to be chaperoned by my nun, but I have a feeling she will remain prostrate and on the verge of fainting until we reach England."

"I thought the same and that is why I have brought you away. Now, beautiful lady, tell me who you are. You already know who I am."

"It sounded very grand and obviously impressed the French official, which was what really mattered."

"And who are you?" he persisted.

"I am Tania Amesly, and my dear father was Lord Amesly. So I am entitled to be called an Honourable too!"

He laughed and it was a very infectious sound.

"For once in our lives," he sighed, "our titles have done the trick and made us important to the French. I have always found, as they have unending collections of Ducs, Marquises, Vicomtes and Comtes that I never stand very high in their estimation."

"Perhaps they just don't understand that an Earl in England is a most illustrious person, but my father always said that the country that really bows low to a long family tree is Germany."

He wrinkled his nose.

"German titles are far too long, too laborious and in my opinion too ugly. You, of course, should be a Princess and everyone would curtsy to you as you are so lovely."

Tania blushed and then she murmured,

"You must not talk to me like that because I find it embarrassing."

"You can hardly expect me to believe that you have not listened to hundreds of compliments already."

"Whether you can believe it or not, I have received practically none because I have only just left school."

The Captain stared at her.

"You have only just left school – how old are you?"

"Well, actually I am over eighteen and should have left long ago, but my stepmother, who does not like me, was determined I should stay as long as possible. Finally the Mother Superior turned me out, so I am going home."

"It's clearly a really sad story. Now do start from the beginning and tell me all about yourself and why your stepmother does not love you as everyone should."

Tania gave a little laugh.

"I would rather hear about you first, Captain. Is it really true you are going home to join your Regiment?"

"It is true, and I am only too glad that I have been able to enjoy this special time in France before being sent off to some outlandish place to fight against the Russians."

As he spoke he thought he had certainly enjoyed himself in France – if it was the last time it would happen, he was extremely glad he had not missed it.

He had gone to France at the invitation of a young Vicomte he had met at Oxford where he had completed his education.

He had not only rowed in the Oxford boat, but had been Captain of the cricket team during his last term.

He had been friends with the Vicomte who was in the same College and he had invited him to stay in Paris with him after Christmas.

Captain More had received special leave from his Commanding Officer and had set off for Paris wondering if he would really enjoy it or if he would have been wiser to stay with friends in England.

As he was an outstanding horseman, he had been invited to hunt with several top packs of foxhounds.

He knew that he could either take his own mounts from his father's stable or be offered those belonging to his hosts.

However, he had gone to Paris and had found it was not only more amusing than he might have expected, but exotic, fantastic and intriguing –

He had never imagined it possible for *courtesans* and *cocottes* to have so much power or give such amusing parties beyond his wildest dreams.

The Vicomte wanted to show him that Paris was far better at amusing a single man than any other City in the world and had taken him from Montmartre to the Champs Elysees, to the *Moulin Rouge* and the *Folies Bergères*.

It was women, women all the time!

Each one more alluring than the last and naturally no less expensive!

Rupert More did not take it particularly seriously, but he enjoyed every moment.

It was only when he realised he must return home to his Regiment that he told himself 'enough is enough'.

Every minute that he had spent in Paris had been a delight, something he would always remember.

There were, however, many other issues of more importance in his life and it was time he attended to them.

He had no wish to go off to war, but even so it was what he had been trained for.

He only hoped that his men, of whom he was very fond, would distinguish themselves on the battlefield.

He was, however, somewhat concerned.

Was the Army, which was being drawn into what would clearly be a very long and bloody campaign, really prepared for what lay ahead?

Unlike a great number of his contemporaries Rupert had always kept up-to-date with politics and he had always been interested in what the diplomats were discussing in every country in Europe.

He was aware, as few young gentlemen in England had bothered to notice, that Great Britain now owned a vast Empire stretching around the world.

One of the most valuable parts of that Empire was India and it was so obvious to Rupert, although no one else seemed to realise it, that if any foreign country threatened the lines of communications from Great Britain to the Far East, that country would have to be repulsed.

His interest in his own country had taught him that Russia possessed a large Empire as well, which embraced eight million square miles, but even that was not enough to prevent the Russians from trying to extend their influence everywhere.

He had also learnt in Paris, if he had not known it before, that the Emperor of France was also ambitious and like other many countries France was mesmerised by the strategic importance of the Middle East.

What was worrying all these three countries at the moment was Turkey.

Having at one time boasted it was 'the Gateway to the East', Turkey had become feeble and was in a perpetual state of general degeneration.

It was, Rupert could see, Turkey's weakness which was encouraging the ambitions of other countries and it seemed obvious that the diplomats should come together and reached agreement between them to prevent war.

But the Czar of Russia, Nicholas I, had spoken of Turkey in a tone of delight,

"*We have on our hands a very sick man*!"

In point of fact, having said that, he had added a recommendation as to how 'the sick man's' property could be disposed of.

When Rupert heard the Czar's comment, it struck him that only a madman would ignore the obvious threats that lay ahead.

If Turkey was to break up, a part of Asia of vitally strategic importance would be open to the other ambitious States and he thought it impossible that England would not recognise this.

The British Cabinet in London should be prepared to thwart the plans that the Czar of Russia was obviously making to seize Turkey.

To Rupert it seemed so imperative that the current situation was calling for a show of strength.

He had been spending a great deal of the night with the most alluring *cocottes* in the whole of Paris and yet he still found time and enough energy in the morning to read all the newspapers.

French newspapers told him that the Czar had sent Prince Menschikov to Turkey as a special Envoy.

Prince Menschikov had arrived with much pomp, accompanied by high-ranking Russian Officers, to demand that the Czar should form in effect a Protectorate over all Christian subjects of the Sultan.

The English were at last aroused by this ambitious move and then hearing that the Turks had been overawed, it was suggested that the British Fleet at Malta should sail to the Dardanelles.

It was obvious to Rupert that this should have been done long before – but better late than never.

The English then persuaded the Sultan of Turkey to state that Russia's proposals would infringe his Sovereign rights and immediately, as he thought otherwise he would look feeble, Prince Menschikov broke off negotiations.

The English next called an international Conference of French, German and Austrian plenipotentiaries.

Menschikov returned to St. Petersburg after telling the Turks to think it over and change their minds.

Rupert supposed that at this moment there would be diplomatic approaches and the great Powers would reach a satisfactory compromise.

To his astonishment the newspapers told him that nothing was done and yet he learned from friends in Paris that the Czar was boiling with indignation.

The newspapers were almost silent for ten days and then they informed the world that Russia had delivered an ultimatum to the Turks – that they must agree to everything the Czar demanded or Russian troops would invade.

It was at this moment that Rupert was recalled to his Regiment.

The newspapers he had bought this morning when he had arrived at the *Gare du Nord* told him that Britain had sent a strong fleet to Besika Bay on the Dardanelles.

'*It is war*! I am sure it is going to be war,' he said to himself.

Now he was sitting beside one of the most beautiful girls he had ever seen.

He hoped, although it was a very forlorn hope, that he might not have to leave London too quickly.

*

It was now late in the afternoon as he and Tania, chattering away happily in the special conveyance they had been given, came into the Station that adjoined the harbour at Boulogne.

The officials on the Station were astonished at the only people occupying their Chief's conveyance were a tall and handsome young man and a very lovely young woman.

They hurried forward to ask what had occurred and Rupert told them in his excellent French that they had been victims of the collision.

They had been sent ahead by the Chief, while the rest of the passengers and the luggage would be arriving in due course.

"Was anyone injured or killed, monsieur?" one of the officials asked.

"I do not think anyone is injured," he replied, "and we were most fortunate to get away so quickly, thanks to your Chief."

It was not too difficult for the officials to realise that Captain More and Tania would not have received such attention unless they were distinguished passengers.

So they were therefore taken straight on board the ferry waiting on the quay.

The Purser, at Rupert's request, gave them the two best cabins available.

"I will see that your luggage is put carefully on one side as soon as it arrives," the Purser offered, "but I would be grateful if you would write your names down clearly so that I cannot make a mistake."

Rupert obliged for both of them.

Then he and Tania asked for something to eat to be brought as soon as possible to their cabins.

It was almost dinner time and Tania was only too glad to take off her hat and coat, tidy her hair and wash her face and hands.

In the meantime Rupert went to find out what was available for dinner and to order a good bottle of wine.

Tania kept thinking how lucky she had been to find someone to look after her after Sister Agnes collapsed.

There was no doubt, she thought, that when one is travelling one needs a man – a woman alone is bound to be ignored or make a mess of anything if she tries to arrange it on her own.

She therefore waited happily for Rupert to return.

When he did, he thought that, without her hat and with her long golden hair framing her lovely face, she was undoubtedly the most beautiful woman he had ever seen.

"Everything is now arranged," he smiled, "and we are going to have a most enjoyable dinner. Although I will not presume to say it aspires to be better than the French would give us."

Tania laughed.

"Papa always said French cooking is unbeatable all over the world. And as he travelled a great deal he knew what he was talking about."

Rupert thought about the exotic meals he had eaten with exotic women this past month and how very costly it had been.

He decided on the whole he was quite content with good plain English fare, but then certainly not with a plain English girl!

He thought Tania was so lovely it was impossible to think of her as being real.

'How,' he asked himself and he was afraid to say it aloud, 'could I possibly have been fortunate enough to find anyone so exquisite – in the middle of a train crash?'

It did seem rather funny and because he laughed out loud, Tania asked him,

"What are you laughing at?"

"Myself," was the reply.

"That is just what we should all do. I have often thought if we were on a stage how funny we would appear and how people would pay to hear us talking and making absurd remarks."

"I never thought of that before, but I am sure you are right and when I think about all those ponderous men in Downing Street and the War Office letting us in for a war, I really think they should have their heads examined."

"Will it be a serious war?" Tania enquired.

"Very serious indeed and frankly I have no wish to kill anyone, not even the Russians."

"Is that what you will have to do?"

"I am a soldier, and soldiers are engaged to fight off anyone who might harm their country."

"And where do you think you will have to fight?"

"I suspect it might be somewhere in South Russia. As you doubtless know, we have to stop the Russians from taking over Turkey which would give them an opening into Asia and eventually carry them as far as India."

"It all seems so far away, Rupert, so it is difficult to realise how important it is and how much it matters to us."

"We may be a small island, but, as you know, our Empire extends over a quarter of the world and we have to protect it and all the people in it like yourself."

"I am so glad that you are protecting me and I very much need protection at the moment!"

"Why?" Rupert asked her sharply.

For a moment she wondered if she should tell him the truth and that she was afraid of her stepmother.

Then she decided to be so serious would spoil the evening as they had both been laughing and talking light-heartedly ever since the train crash.

And she was quite certain that this stranger was not really interested in her private affairs.

"What I would really like, Rupert, is for you to tell me about your time in Paris and if you found it enjoyable as everyone always says it is."

"Who have you been listening to, Tania?"

"The girls at school told me what fun their brothers had going to places of entertainment in Montmartre and to parts of Paris where they would not take their sisters, and where I, as an English girl, would never be allowed to go."

Rupert knew this was true and a good thing too.

It would spoil anything so lovely, so untouched and so innocent as the glorious girl facing him.

He had thought when he first saw her that she was the most beautiful creature he had ever set eyes on.

Now he realised he had known instinctively that she was so very different from the women he had spent his holiday with.

He was sure that she was intelligent and yet there was an innocence about her that told him she had no idea of how some other women behaved.

Or of the entertainments that men found so amusing but would never allow in their own home nor permit their daughters to take part in.

'What this girl is surely looking for,' he mused, 'is someone who will love her completely and absolutely, and never find anything more exciting than the softness of her lips and the exquisite smoothness of her skin.'

Then as Tania looked at him enquiringly, he told himself,

'I said I will look after her and protect her and that I must do, even though it might mean protecting her against myself!'

CHAPTER TWO

When they had finished dinner, they went on deck to see if there was any sign of the others arriving from the damaged train.

There was a train coming in, but as soon as he saw it Rupert remarked,

"That train is not the one we are expecting."

"How do you know?" asked Tania.

"Because I can see it has come from Germany."

She thought that he must have a very astute mind as to be honest all the trains looked the same to her.

When the train drew up above them in the Station, she could see that it was not very long and unless it was totally packed in every carriage it could not have carried all the passengers who were on their train from Paris.

"We will be very late leaving," Tania whispered.

"I am quite content to be here talking to you – " he replied.

The train came to a standstill and then a number of the ferry Stewards went up to the Station.

"They must have been delayed as well. Surely we should have left by now?" Tania asked.

"You can never be sure with Continental trains and for one thing, the ferries do not wish to waste their coal and energy taking only a few passengers across to England.

"This boat will, I am certain, be packed solid before

it finally sails and we are so fortunate to have secured the best available cabins before anyone else could."

"I believe there are only a very few private cabins on these ferries," Tania added.

She thought that she was lucky to have someone so interesting and so handsome to talk to.

At her school Tania had naturally met the brothers of the girls she was friendly with and she had been invited frequently to their homes for the holidays.

She had stayed away in French, Spanish and Italian houses, but because she was only a schoolgirl, the brothers of the other girls paid little attention to her.

She formed the distinct impression that they were heavily engaged with some fascinating women who would not be acceptable to their mothers.

Anyway the young men came and went and were not interested in a mere schoolgirl.

Now, she thought, she had had a really interesting conversation with the tall handsome man beside her.

"Here they come!" he cried, leaning over the rail. "And I hope you will be pleased to see there are not very many of them."

Tania thought that if the train had been full when it had left Germany then many of the passengers would have got out further up the line.

They would not know until they reached the scene of the accident that the railway line had been blocked.

Nevertheless from her point of view it was useful that there were only twenty or thirty people now boarding the ferry.

Then, as a couple walking rather more slowly than the others, came down the steps which led to the gangway, suddenly Tania gave a little cry.

"Oh, over there! There are some friends of mine!" she exclaimed. "It is so exciting to see them and you must come to meet them, Rupert."

She had a feeling, although she was not sure, that the handsome Captain beside her was disappointed that she had found some friends so unexpectedly.

Although he did not say so, she was quite right.

He was enjoying having this beautiful young girl all to himself and had no wish for her to be caught up with her friends.

However, he could hardly refuse to go below as she insisted.

They went down from the upper deck just as the train party was moving slowly into the ship – most of them were First Class and were directed to the main deck.

It was then as Tania saw Mr. and Mrs. Bracebridge come aboard that she gave another cry of delight and ran towards them.

She had first met the Bracebridges many years ago when she was very young. She had often visited their most impressive house in Belgrave Square with her parents.

She had even once stayed at their delightful country home – Atherstone Hall near Coventry.

She knew that they were very rich but childless and they had always made a great fuss of her and her parents had been very fond of them both.

Mrs. Bracebridge was tall, stately and beautiful and Tania's mother had said once that, as well as being artistic and intelligent, she had the greatest warmth of character of anyone she had ever known.

She recalled, as she waited while they spoke to the Captain of the ferry, that Charles Bracebridge was a well-known traveller and owned property in Athens.

"He is generous, impetuous and often petulant," her father had said. "He has huge pride in his family and has traced their descent back from Lady Godiva!"

What her father had liked more than anything else was Charles Bracebridge's horses. He had brought many back from the Far East and had bred from them.

Of course her father had ridden his horses and had frequently stayed at Atherstone Hall for their amusing and entertaining parties.

Now when they had finished being greeted by the Captain, as they were obviously of great importance, Tania ran towards them.

Before she reached them, Mrs. Bracebridge threw out her hands and exclaimed,

"Tania, what on earth are you doing here?"

"I am on my way home," Tania answered as she kissed Mrs. Bracebridge, "and then my train smashed into another. It was only by good fortune that I managed to get here and did not have to wait until they could move all the other passengers."

"You are not alone?" Charles Bracebridge asked as he kissed her.

"No, and please let me introduce Captain More who has been very kind to me."

Charles Bracebridge put out his hand.

"I would not have expected you to be here either, Rupert," he chuckled. "I thought you would be on your way to Turkey."

"That is just what I was expecting myself," he said, "but it is delightful to see you again, Mr. Bracebridge. I have not forgotten how much I enjoyed riding your Arab horses the last time I was at Atherstone."

"Well, do let's sit down somewhere whilst you tell us all the excitements," Mrs. Bracebridge now suggested.

"I understand that we have a cabin and I'm sure we will be much more comfortable there than anywhere else."

"We also have cabins, so we will all be together," Tania told her. "I am very happy I will not have to share it with the old nun who was supposed to be looking after me. But she completely collapsed when our train crashed."

"I have never heard such a dramatic story," gushed Mrs. Bracebridge. "So let's go now to our cabins and you must tell us everything right from the beginning."

They moved up to the cabins on the upper deck and Tania found to her delight that the Bracebridge cabin was only one door away from hers – and that one was Rupert's.

"You were terribly lucky to get these cabins," Mrs. Bracebridge prattled on. "We always book far ahead, but I don't suppose you had booked yours."

"No, we just arrived," replied Tania. "But because they were so impressed with Captain More, we were lucky enough to book a cabin each and we have just finished our dinner."

"Well, my lady's maid will be along in a moment," Mrs. Bracebridge said, "and the rest of our luggage will arrive when the porters move it from the guard's van."

"I will see to it," Charles offered, "and don't worry! Take Tania into your cabin and order us some champagne. I am sure Rupert will be only too pleased to join us."

"I suppose I really should not be that surprised to see you as you are always travelling," said Rupert. "I only think it strange that your great friend Florence Nightingale is not with you."

He was well aware that Selina Bracebridge prided herself in collecting most interesting people. In particular she enjoyed young writers and musicians.

The Nightingale family had hoped that Selina, who was so happily married and a firm believer in matrimony, would persuade young Florence to accept a distinguished and handsome man who was longing to make her his wife.

But so far she had been unsuccessful.

They had taken Florence on many of their tours of Europe and yet she was still convinced that she should not marry, but wait for the special mission she believed would be sent to her by God.

She had, however, travelled with the Bracebridges to Egypt and then to Greece in 1840.

She had written endless letters home to her mother describing how much she enjoyed the experience and being with the Bracebridges.

They were entertained by Governors, Ambassadors, Consul-Generals and all the most distinguished people in every country they visited.

But this got Florence Nightingale no nearer, much to her family's dismay, to accepting marriage with Richard Monckton Milnes who later became Lord Houghton.

Tania had heard this story from her mother and in fact she had been most impressed that any young woman, because she believed she had a vocation, should refuse the man she claimed she 'adored'.

Now as she reached her cabin, Tania enquired,

"You were just going to tell me all about Florence Nightingale. I often thought about her at school. You will remember I met her once with you at your lovely house in Belgrave Square."

"Florence has done a great deal since then!" cried Selina. "I don't know if you have been told that she has gained her first nursing experience in Germany."

"I think I remember Papa saying something about it before I was sent off to school, but I have been there for two years and only now am I at last going home, although

Stepmama begged the Mother Superior to keep me there even longer."

"I never heard such a thing. Of course you should have come out last year and that is exactly what I thought had happened, but we were away and were extremely upset when we learnt that your father had died."

"I was not even able to say goodbye to him," Tania whispered with tears welling up in her eyes.

Selina was about to speak, but then drew her lips together.

She had always disliked the second Lady Amesly, but had understood that Tania's father was very unhappy and lonely when his wife died.

He had therefore succumbed to the very determined onslaught made upon him by Isobel.

But she had no idea that she was unkind and what really amounted to being cruel to poor Tania.

She evaded an uncomfortable moment by saying,

"My friend Florence is at the moment really happy as she is now in charge of a small hospital in Harley Street.

"It is named '*The Institution for the Care of Sick Gentlewomen in Distressed Circumstances*.' To be honest the name is longer than the place itself! But needless to say she has been a huge success there and I hope you will be able to see her now you are returning to England."

"I should love to meet her again and I am so happy to see you here, Mrs. Bracebridge."

"I sent you a Christmas present, Tania, but I had no idea you were not be at home and I would suppose that you never received it."

"No, or I would have thanked you. My Stepmama's secretary wrote to tell me that various presents had arrived in London, but it would be a nuisance to have to send them on. So she said they must wait until I return home."

"She has obviously not been in a hurry to let you do so if you say you are over eighteen?"

"She does not want me around at all and I am just wondering what I will do when I do reach home."

"Perhaps it will not be as bad as all that, my dear. After all, you are looking very much like your dear Mama and very pretty. I am sure you will be asked to many balls. In fact, I will make sure that your parents' friends know that you have returned."

"That is so kind of you, and it will be nice to go to balls and meet people of my own age."

"I see you have already met one handsome young man," smiled Selina.

Rupert and Charles, having ordered the champagne, had walked out on deck, leaving Selina and Tania alone in the cabin.

It was a double one and therefore much bigger than Tania's. Besides two bunks there were chairs and a table for the champagne.

"I hope," Selina asked when the men came in, "that we will not have to wait here very long."

"I am afraid you are being a bit over-optimistic, my dear," replied Charles. "As far as I can learn there is no sign yet of anyone from the railway accident and I doubt if the ferry will sail without them."

"I was just telling Tania about dear Florence – "

"I am interested too," added Rupert. "I have heard people talking about your friend, Florence Nightingale, and how brilliantly she has managed the hospital in London."

"Who told you that?" asked Selina.

"My late mother was a member of a charitable trust headed by Lady Canning, who told her a long time ago that a new superintendent was needed and another friend, Lady Petheridge, had put forward Miss Nightingale's name."

"I am not surprised you heard that," added Charles. "Florence has run it brilliantly and every single patient has left praising her up to the skies.

"She is worth fifty doctors and has more common sense than they ever expected to find in a woman!"

They all laughed and Tania knew it was something very strange for a woman to be in charge of sick people.

In essence it was quite a sensation.

As if Selina guessed her thoughts, she remarked,

"Florence's main difficulty is to find nurses. There are absolutely none who are properly trained and as you can imagine the doctors are not at all helpful.

She paused thoughtfully and then commented,

"I am just wondering, if we go to war with Russia, what she will want to do about such a serious problem."

"You know the answer to that," said her husband. "But she will not find it at all easy to be accepted on the battlefield."

"I just cannot believe that we will really go to war!" exclaimed Selina.

"I'm afraid that there will be no alternative," Rupert told her. "We all know the Russians have been exceedingly tiresome lately."

"At the same time it seems such a long way away, and I cannot believe that you or any soldier would want to fight a war in a climate that is too hot in the summer and too cold in the winter."

"It is what we will have to put up with unless the Russians give way and I just cannot see them doing that."

"The trouble with those foreigners is that they find it impossible to lose face," Charles declared. "And we can only hope that by some miracle peace will come and save us at the last moment."

As they finished their champagne Selina was telling Tania how much Florence Nightingale had enjoyed their journey to Rome.

"I am sure you would love to go there yourself, my dear. Florence wrote to me that she had never enjoyed any time in her life as much as when she was in Rome."

"I can understand. Mama always spoke of Rome as one of the most beautiful places she had ever seen."

"Florence spent a whole day in the Sistine Chapel with me staring up at the '*Heaven of Angels and Prophets'*. She also loved the journey to Egypt and we meant to take her with us this time to Berlin, but she was far too busy."

"If there is a war," commented Tania, "I'm sure she will want to care for the wounded."

"That is what my husband has been saying to me all the time we have been travelling and I am convinced that anything I may say to dissuade her will fall on deaf ears."

They sat talking for a little while longer until Selina said she felt tired and must to retire to bed.

Tania quickly rose and kissed her goodnight.

"I apologise, Mrs. Bracebridge, for staying so long but it is so wonderful to talk to you and to remember how fond my parents were of you and your husband."

"I am glad I am not forgotten," Charles added. "I always thought your mother was one of the most beautiful women I have ever seen. I know you will be pleased when I say that you are very like her."

"Thank you," replied Tania, "that is a compliment I really appreciate. If I am half as lovely and clever as my Mama, I will be content."

She and Rupert left the cabin together.

When they were outside, he suggested,

"Let's go and see if the others have arrived yet."

They walked to the other side of the ferry.

The lights were still burning brightly and there was some activity at the Station, but there was no sign of the crowds who were expected to come from the train crash.

"I am so sorry for those poor people," Tania sighed, "but you would not have thought it would have taken them so long to rush a relief train to the accident."

"I don't know, Tania, I fancy it would take a long time especially as they had to manhandle all that luggage. I only hope mine is not left behind."

"I hope the same and of course we are being selfish. But I am very very grateful that you rescued me."

"And I am delighted I did so and now that you are being properly chaperoned by one of your Mama's friends, you need not feel guilty of coming away with me when I suggested it."

"I didn't feel guilty – merely very grateful because you had been so kind."

"Just how could I be anything else when, as Mrs. Bracebridge has already told you, you are *so* beautiful. In fact I expect you will take London by storm."

"I think you are being over-optimistic."

"But I would like to point out that I found you first! Thus I feel not only privileged, but someone who deserves more than those who may come after me!"

Tania laughed.

"Now you are making me feel very important and that is what I want to feel when, as you realise, I am really too old to be a *debutante*. Perhaps when I do reach London no one will want to bother with me."

"I think you are greatly under-estimating yourself, I, for one, will want to see you, to dance with you and I am determined to spend as much time as I can with you before I am sent away into the back of beyond."

There was a silence before Tania asked him,

"Are you quite certain that if there is a war you will have to go to it?"

"Of course I want to take part in it, but I only wish it was not in that particular part of the world, and I am also hoping that the British Army is ready for a war which may be an extremely bitter one."

"Why do you say that?"

"I would not say that to a foreigner, but it is well-known that the Army over the past few years ever since the Battle of Waterloo has been run down and scandalously neglected."

He spoke with an obvious bitterness, which made it impossible not to believe that he was speaking the truth.

"Surely you are being pessimistic, Rupert. I always believed that our Army is the pride of the country and we need its strength to protect our great Empire."

"That is just what it ought to be, but for thirty-nine years the Army has been neglected and the victim of gross economy. I am exceedingly worried now as to whether we have enough arms to fight – apart from anything else."

"But surely you should speak to someone about it?"

"My father would have done that if he had not been in ill health and unable to take up the post that was offered to him in the Cabinet. He has said over and over again that the whole organisation should be brought up-to-date.

"But he was speaking from his sick bed, so no one was likely to listen to him."

Because he seemed so upset, Tania put out her hand and laid it on his arm.

"I am sure it will not be as bad as you fear it will be and if the war actually does come, the British will wake up and, as they always do, win the battle."

"That I am prepared to believe, but it may be at the expense of a large number of men being killed who might otherwise have lived. We have nothing like the numbers of trained soldiers that we should have."

Realising he should not be saying this to a young girl, he forced himself to add in a different tone of voice,

"This does not concern you, Tania. All you have to do is to be lovely and make us men happy before we go to war and welcome us back with open arms if and when we return."

"I believe every woman who cares for England will do so, but I am very worried by what you have just said."

"Then it's a big mistake for me to have said it," he muttered. "What we must do now is to plan how you can enjoy yourself, having missed a Season in London, before I leave, if I do have to, for Turkey."

Tania felt an excitement within her she had never known before.

"Do you really mean it?" she asked him. "Will I see you again when we reach London?"

"I have every intention of seeing you, Tania, and I intend to tell all my relatives – and I have quite a number of them – that they must open their doors to you so that you can accept their hospitality."

"Which I will be most happy to do, kind sir. You do realise that being cooped up at school, even though they were very kind to me, is not the same as being allowed to be grown-up and to attend the endless balls and parties that I understand always make a *debutante's* Season."

"Nothing is ever too late to mend. Now, before we worry about the war or anything else, we must worry about *you* and how organised you must be."

Tania thought at the back of her mind that if there was any organising to do, it would be her stepmother who should do it.

At the same time she was hoping against hope that this charming young man would not forget his promise to her when he arrived in London.

It was then that they heard the puffing of a train and slowly one came into the Station above them.

"They have arrived at last. Now we will be able to start our voyage back to England."

Even as Rupert spoke there was a babble of voices and a few moments later the first passengers were hurrying down to the ferry.

Tania knew the Third Class passengers who could not afford a cabin were determined, if nothing else, to find the best seat obtainable.

She could see Sister Agnes being helped along by the other nun and felt relieved that at least she was being adequately looked after.

She and Rupert watched as the eager crowd surged further down the gangway and into the ferry.

*

It was almost an hour later that Tania remarked,

"We will be sailing pretty soon, as the engines are already turning, so I think we should now retire to bed."

"But I have no wish to say 'goodnight'," objected Rupert.

"We will see each other tomorrow, Rupert."

"I know, Tania, but I expect the Bracebridges will be with us and I want you to myself."

She looked up at him.

As their eyes met, they were both very still.

"It is too soon, and I know we have only just met each other," Rupert said in a low voice, "but I do feel that something very significant has occurred to both of us."

Tania drew in her breath.

"I hope you are right," she whispered, "but I have only just met you."

"I do not think that is quite true. I feel sure I have met you before, perhaps in another life, which in the East they all believe in."

He was silent for a moment and then he added,

"Perhaps it was just in my dreams I met someone as lovely as you."

Tania felt shy.

"Thank – you," she breathed. "But as you said – it is too soon to talk about it."

The words came jerkily from between her lips.

Because she was not certain of herself, she ran over the deck to her cabin.

As she opened the door, she turned back,

"And goodnight, Rupert, and thank you very much for your kindness."

She went in and closed the door.

Then she stood for a moment with her hands up to her cheeks.

How was it possible that any man she had just met could make her feel as she felt now?

Then she told herself that the sooner she climbed into bed and tried to sleep, the sooner she would see him again in the morning.

She wished she had not run away from him.

Now it was too late.

Even as she thought about it she heard his footsteps cross the deck and the door of his cabin close.

'He is so exciting and different from anyone I have ever met,' she pondered.

After all she had been away for two years, and she was only sixteen when she had gone to the French school.

Although parties had been held for her at home they had been children's parties – with children's games.

Now she wanted to dance and to feel she was not a *debutante* but a woman.

When she climbed into bed, she said her prayers as she always did and she thanked God for bringing Captain Rupert More into her life and that he would remember his promise to her.

When finally she fell asleep, it was to dream that she was dancing a waltz in the moonlight.

Rupert was with her, but he was not touching her in her dream and somehow she wanted him to.

*

In his own cabin Rupert was thinking about Tania.

At the very same time he was worrying what would actually happen if, as he thought inevitable, England went to war.

As his father had said so often, the worst thing was the inefficient system at the War Office.

"You can say what you like, Rupert," he had said the last time he had been at home, "but the chief problem of this country, if we are at war, will not be in beating the enemy, but organising a force that would be a credit to us."

"You have told me so often, Papa," Rupert replied, "that the Army has been run down and neglected."

"I have said it so often to so many people, but they pay no attention. Mark my words the rot is there from top to bottom."

Because Rupert was intelligent, he knew his father was not exaggerating the ineffective system of control.

The Secretary of State for War was responsible for the Army and he was assisted by the Minister for War.

It was he who took the Government's decisions to the Commander-in-Chief of the Army, a General whose Headquarters was in Horse Guards.

The Major-General of Ordinance was not a soldier, as might have been expected, but a Member of Parliament.

He controlled procurement of military equipment, weapons, supply of food for the troops and the engineers and artillery.

Another department was that of the Commissioner responsible for our troops abroad, which came under the Treasury.

There had been many complaints, to which no one had ever attended, about the food and the Medical Board and a dozen other departments that were badly organised.

It was Rupert's father who kept on pointing at two most essential and proved units that had been abolished at the end of the Napoleonic wars.

They were the Wagon Train and the Staff Corps – both essential after a campaign had taken place.

"It is the incredibly rapid demobilisation that came immediately after the Battle of Waterloo which will defeat us now as we have never been defeated before," the Earl of Grantmore had declared over and over again.

Now his son was wondering if it would be as bad as his father feared. If so, was it too late to do anything about it?

Just before Rupert fell asleep he was thinking not so much of the war, but of Tania.

She had appeared just after the train crash looking like an angel who had just dropped down from Heaven.

'She is entrancing, she is so beautiful and whatever happens I must not lose sight of her,' he told himself.

He realised that under present circumstances it was very unlikely that he would be long in England.

Once he was abroad there would be plenty of eager men, he was quite certain, who would be ready to take his place at her side.

'*At least,*' he lectured himself before he finally fell asleep, 'I will be sure of seeing her while I am in London.'

He was almost certain that the Cavalry would not be going out to Turkey right away.

He would therefore be able to spend some of his time, when he was not actively training his troops, with the lovely girl he had found in a wrecked train.

*

When he awoke the next morning, Rupert realised they were still at sea and it was rough.

The ferry was pitching and tossing and as the waves broke over the bow, it was making slow progress across the Channel.

He reckoned with a sinking heart that Tania would be lying prostrate and seasick and it would be impossible to talk to her.

Going to her cabin, he knocked gently at the door.

He did not expect an answer, but to his surprise she called out to come in.

He found that she was up and dressed.

"Good morning, Rupert, I rather expected that you would sleep in longer and be worried about going on deck in case you were blown away or soaked with foam!"

"And I was thinking you would be prostrate with seasickness!"

Tania laughed.

"As it happens I am a good sailor. I was in a huge storm once with Papa and everybody was sick except him and me, even the crew looked a bit green. But we enjoyed every moment of it."

"It is what I might have expected, Tania, and would you like your breakfast here or down below."

"Here, if they do condescend to bring it up and we must be careful not to wake up our neighbours."

She smiled as she added,

"Even though they are great travellers, I was told Mrs. Bracebridge hates a rough sea."

"Two very sensible people – "

"I think it is so beautiful when the sea is rough and I am always certain I can spy mermaids in the foam."

Rupert chuckled.

"What do you want for breakfast? I had better go and order it, as I am certain the Stewards will think we are too ill to want to eat anything."

"Eggs and bacon and coffee, please."

He smiled at Tania.

"You are magnificent! I might have known it if I had any common sense."

"Why do you say that?"

"Because you are completely unique, Tania. Only a unique woman, so different from any others I have ever met, would survive a train crash, a rough sea and what may lie ahead of us – a war."

"Now you are being pessimistic again, Rupert, I am hoping that at the last moment we will find a way to keep the peace. Actually I have put it in my prayers."

"In which case they will undoubtedly come true, if there were not a large number of other people praying that, as the war is essential for the future of the British Empire, we will win it!"

"But of course we will, Rupert. Even though you did worry me last night with your gloomy forebodings that the Army has no weapons and doubtless no soldiers!"

She was joking, but as Rupert went below to order breakfast, he thought maybe it was a joke that could end up as reality.

After he had given the order and was walking back to Tania's cabin he was thinking again how lovely she was.

He was therefore not surprised to find her standing outside leaning over the rail, watching the waves breaking over the bow.

The sun was shining on the sea and glittering on the foam from the breaking waves – it was like looking into the heart of a rainbow.

When Rupert joined her, she looked up and smiled.

"This is yet another adventure," she sighed, "and I thought we should reach home without one."

"Do you really like a rough sea, Tania?"

"I like the feeling that something is happening and that we are fighting a battle against the elements and in the end we will win it."

He could see from her eyes that she was referring not only to what was happening now but to the future.

"Of course we will win, as Britain always does. It is just that I am wondering how much it would all cost us in money and men."

"What you must tell your men, Rupert, is that they are fighting for a just cause, and if they do die it is for the glory of England and not just to contain a greedy gesture on the part of the Russians."

"You are so right, Tania and, of course, '*to hear is to obey*'."

He smiled as he quoted the Arab saying and Tania smiled back at him.

"I was thinking just now, Rupert, how exciting it was meeting you. Not at all what one would expect in the middle of a train crash."

"Funnily enough, Tania, I was thinking exactly the same about you before I went to sleep. I am therefore quite certain you are not human, but have been sent down here from the sky especially to intrigue and entrance me!"

Tania clapped her hands together.

"That is a wonderful idea and so very romantic. If you can talk like that, you should put it into a poem or a book and when it is published you will make a fortune!"

"It's most unlikely, and although my father always keeps his diary day by day and often talks about writing his life story, it has never particularly attracted me."

"We are too young at present to have realised what an exciting world we are living in, where strange things are happening and new things being invented! But war should be abolished altogether."

"Then we would not be living here in England, but in Heaven where everyone loves everyone else and no one wants to fight."

"It is something we must work for, Rupert."

"Maybe you will be successful, like that person you were talking about to Mrs. Bracebridge."

"Oh, you mean Florence Nightingale. She believes she has something very special to do for the world that has never been done before by anybody."

"Then I suppose we could all try to do the same. If I have to bring peace, what do *you* intend to do, Tania?"

"I was just thinking about that myself. If you give the world peace and Florence gives the world good health, then I must in some way, though I am uncertain how, give the world *love*."

"That is exactly the right answer, Tania!"

CHAPTER THREE

It was late in the afternoon before finally the ferry, rather battered by the rough sea, drew into London Bridge.

The Bracebridges had hardly left their cabin all day.

On the top deck the only people moving about were Tania and Rupert.

He had always been a good sailor and a rough sea did not worry him – in fact he rather enjoyed it.

But he had never known a woman who enjoyed it too and Tania was proving to be even more unique than he at first thought her to be.

They decided to take luncheon together in Tania's cabin as they were not invited by the Bracebridges.

Tania knew this was because Mrs. Bracebridge was feeling seasick and her husband wanted to be with her.

He had come out once or twice to see if they were all right and was rather amused to see they were enjoying the storm.

Despite the heavy sea there was no rain and the sun was shining for most of the afternoon.

Rupert went below and returned to say that nearly all the passengers were seasick and Stewards were running from one to the other as quickly as they could.

Tania now felt concerned that Sister Agnes would be suffering on the lower deck, but there was really nothing she could do to help her.

When they finally steamed into the Thames, it was already dusk but they were no longer being tossed about.

Mrs. Bracebridge, who had been lying all day in her bed, finally got up and dressed.

"Can I give you any help?" Tania asked her.

She shook her head.

"I am all right now, thank you, Tania. Although I have not actually been sick, a rough sea always gives me a terrible headache and I know it's wiser to stay in bed."

"I think it is so sensible of you, but the poor people below unfortunately have only seats to sit on and they must have suffered terribly as they were so seasick."

"They will soon recover," Charles said cheerfully, "and I must commend you and Rupert for being such good sailors."

Charles had arranged that their luggage was to be the first to be taken off the ship.

Tania was not at all surprised to find that there was no carriage waiting for her.

She thought, if her stepmother had sent one at her expected time of arrival, it had certainly not waited.

"Never mind, my dear," Selina had said. "There is plenty of room in our carriage and we can give both you and Rupert a lift. If you will drop us first, the carriage can then take you on to wherever you want to go."

"You are so kind," Tania thanked her. "I hate to be a nuisance, but I have a distinct feeling that Stepmama will be convinced that it is my fault we are so late!"

They laughed at this, but Rupert knew she meant it seriously and he was worried.

He had already recognised that Tania would not be welcomed home by her stepmother and wanted to protect her from being made unhappy and scolded for what was certainly not her fault.

They travelled first to Belgrave Square where the Bracebridges said 'goodbye' to them both and then as she was climbing out of the carriage, Selina held up her hand,

"What I would suggest, and I might have thought of it earlier, is that you must both of you come and dine with us tomorrow night. I will ask some of your mother's great friends, Tania. I know they will be thrilled to see you and the word will soon go round that you are back in London."

"I would just love to and I am so glad I was able to meet you in such an unexpected way."

"I look forward to seeing you too," Charles said to Rupert. "And tell your father when you see him that I want to be in touch with him at the first opportunity."

"I know he is in London at the moment, because he is receiving special medical treatment. He is in our house in Park Lane and I can tell you without asking him how delighted he will be to see you."

"I never thought of him in London, as I know how much he enjoys the country and particularly his horses and I never suspected he would leave them."

"His doctors insisted he should take this treatment in London. So I will tell him to expect you just as soon as you have recovered from your journey."

"I will be calling on him without fail tomorrow or the next day and don't forget that we expect you to dinner tomorrow night."

"I am not likely to forget it," answered Rupert, "and thank you again for everything."

The footman asked Tania where to go and she gave him the address of her father's house in Park Lane.

It was, she thought, only a short way from Rupert's.

She was hoping that he would be as anxious to call on her as Charles Bracebridge was to call on his father.

As they drove off with Rupert sitting beside her, he took her hand in both of his and suggested,

"Though we will see each other at dinner tomorrow night, I will try to call on you in the afternoon, but sadly it may not be possible."

"You mean you will be busy at your Barracks?"

As she felt suddenly afraid he might be sent away from England without any notice, she added,

"This war has not yet started, so surely there is still a chance of peace."

"I would rather doubt it, Tania. We can only pray that someone has a little common sense before there is a mass slaughter. I imagine the majority of soldiers on both sides will have no idea what they are fighting for."

"Naturally they would feel like that if the enemy is not invading their own land, and I am sorry for the Turks, who will suffer more than anyone else."

Rupert did not answer and after a while she added,

"I hope you will be able to have dinner tomorrow night with those kind Bracebridges. It was so fortunate for me that we bumped into them, just as I was so lucky that you looked after me when the trains crashed."

"We must hope that your luck continues, Tania, and I am quite certain, because you are so beautiful, that it will. At the same time I hope if I am sent abroad immediately, you will not forget me."

"How could I possibly? It has all been an adventure I never thought could ever happen to me. When we were watching the waves I felt how marvellous it all was."

"And I thought it was so wonderful that you were there beside me," Rupert breathed.

As he was speaking, he picked up her hand and to her surprise kissed it.

She had taken off her gloves to bid 'goodbye' to the Bracebridges and had not put them on again.

Now as she felt Rupert's lips on the softness of her skin, she felt a little quiver go through her.

But before she could speak the horses slowed down and they were outside her home.

As the footman jumped down from the box to ring the bell, she whispered quickly,

"If you cannot come and see me tomorrow, please will you somehow let me know?"

"If I do come tomorrow, it will be after tea, but if it's impossible, nothing will prevent me from seeing you at dinner."

As she spoke the door of the house opened and he kissed her hand again swiftly and released it.

The footman then opened the carriage door.

"Thank you for everything," murmured Tania.

She would have got out of the carriage, but Rupert jumped out first and helped her alight.

He escorted her to the front door saying,

"Sleep well, Tania, and do not forget our plans for tomorrow."

"I most certainly will not."

She smiled at the butler who she had known since she was a child.

"I am back home, Dawson."

"And I'm real glad to see you, Miss Tania. When the carriage comes back to say the ship had been delayed we were afraid there'd been an accident."

"It was not the ship that had the accident, but the train!"

Dawson gave a sigh of relief.

"I'm just sorry, Miss Tania, that the carriage wasn't waiting for you when you arrived. But her Ladyship were adamant that the coachman shouldn't go out again."

"I rather suspected that, but fortunately I was given a lift by two friends who were very kind to me."

"I'm ever so glad, miss."

While they were talking, two footmen had brought her luggage into the house.

"Is her Ladyship in?" she asked Dawson.

"No, Miss Tania. She's gone out to a party and I doubts if she'll be back afore the early hours."

Tania felt a sense of relief.

"In which case I will go straight up to my room."

Dawson did not reply to her and she looked at him in surprise.

"Is there any reason for me not to do so?"

"No, Miss Tania, but I be afraid that her Ladyship's changed your room."

"Changed my room! But I've slept there ever since I was old enough to leave the nursery."

"I knows that, miss, and I knows it would upset you but her Ladyship wants the best rooms for her friends when they come to stay. So you've been put upstairs in the night nursery."

Tania stared at him in astonishment.

The night nursery had been empty for years or only used by visiting servants.

Everything in her own room had been chosen for her very carefully by her mother and she never imagined for a minute that it would be given to someone else.

For a moment she considered insisting on going to the room she had always used.

But she knew if she did so her stepmother would be furious not only with her but with the servants who had permitted her to do so.

"Very well, Dawson," she said, "but it is a strange homecoming when I cannot even go to my own room."

"I know, Miss Tania, and we all knows it'd upset you, but there be nothing we can do about it."

"I know. So my luggage had better go up into the nursery, but I will not start unpacking until I have talked to her Ladyship about the arrangement."

She saw by the expression on Dawson's face that he did not think anything she did would make very much difference.

She had an uncomfortable feeling in her heart that this was true.

She was, however, affectionately greeted by the old housekeeper who, like Dawson, had been with her father and mother for many years.

She was to learn later that the rest of the servants were all newcomers.

"Now I'm sure you'd like something to eat," the housekeeper – Mrs. Field suggested, "and I've persuaded cook to make the mushroom soup you always loved. She's also cooking you a piece of fresh sole that came from the fishmonger only this morning."

"That will be lovely, Mrs. Field, and as I am now confined to the nursery I had better eat it at the table where Nanny taught me to have good manners and always to say grace before I ate."

She thought as she spoke it would be wise to be grateful for small mercies, even though this was hardly a happy way to return home.

She longed to go to her Mama's room and feel that she was still there.

She would understand how strange it was to come home to find that everything had been altered, but she was afraid that her mother's room would be changed too.

In which case it would be most hurtful to see the alterations and to know they were her stepmother's choice.

Perhaps this had all been done deliberately – as the new Lady Amesly would want to erase all the memories of someone who had been more loved than she had ever been.

Tania could remember her stepmother raging at her father and blustering,

"I have done everything to make you happy, and all you think about is that woman who is dead and can never return! Forget her! Forget her and think of me! I am your wife and you should not be thinking of anyone else!"

Tania had not been there when her stepmother had said all this – she had been in the next room and the door had been slightly ajar.

She had not waited to hear her father's answer.

She had run off to her own room because she could not bear to hear anyone speak in such a way of her beloved Mama and at the same time upsetting her Papa.

'Why did he ever marry such a woman?' she had asked herself when she was alone.

It was the same question she repeated over and over again as time passed.

*

Now when she walked into the nursery, it was all so familiar. She only wished that Nanny, who had loved and spoilt her, was there as well.

Nothing had been changed from when she had been a child.

The rocking horse was in front of the window and the screen on which Nanny had stuck their Christmas cards they received each year was by the fireplace and her doll's house, sadly dilapidated, was propped up in one corner.

A maid she had never seen before came forward rather disdainfully to ask if she wished to have anything unpacked.

"Only what is in my night case. Leave the trunks until tomorrow, as I may not be staying in this room – "

The maid gave her a sideways glance and it told her that it would be highly unlikely that she would be able to alter her stepmother's strict instructions.

The maid opened her case and put her nightgown on the bed that had already been turned down.

Tania took off her coat and hat and then she went to the window of the nursery.

Leaning over the rocking horse she looked out into the garden at the back of the house.

She remembered so well how she had played there happily when her mother was alive.

She had gone to a day school in London when she grew too old to be taught by a Governess, and then as soon as her father married again, she had been sent to school in France and had not been allowed home.

When her father began to suffer from ill health, he had been unable to resist the many excuses her stepmother had made to keep her away – without even hearing them Tania knew all too well what had been said.

Most of all she would feel homesick again, as she had been at first and would beg her father to let her come home and be educated in London.

It was jealousy that had made her stepmother resent the love and every kindness her father gave her.

Tania thought it was because she hoped that the less Lord Amesly saw of his daughter, the less he would leave her in his will and this, of course, would mean there would be so much more for his wife.

Tania realised that she was extremely grasping and greedy when it came to money.

She decided that, now she was back in London, the first thing she should do was to see exactly what money of her own she had in the bank.

Her father had written to her when he was not at all well to explain,

"*I have made provision for you in my will and if, my dearest, anything does happen to me, Mr. Sinworth at Sinworth, Mores and Lambeth will look after you and see that you have everything I want you to have.*"

His writing looked distinctly faint and the envelope had been addressed by Dawson and Tania had suspected it had been sent to her without her stepmother's knowledge.

'I am sure she will grasp everything she can,' Tania mused, 'and if possible leave me penniless.'

When finally she went to bed, she thought that the mattress was not as soft as it had been in her own room.

The austerity of the night nursery was so different from the room her mother had given her next to hers.

If her stepmother had moved her into another room on the first floor Tania might have understood, but to send her up to the nursery was to make it so obvious she was no longer welcome in her own home.

'What shall I do? What on earth shall I do?' she asked herself desperately.

Then almost as if God was answering the cry which came from her heart, she recalled that Selina Bracebridge had offered to help her.

'I am frightened, I am very frightened, Mama,' she murmured to the darkness before she went to sleep. 'But I feel wherever you and Papa are, you will look after me and when I pray you will be near me.'

The prayer came from the very depths of her heart.

Only when she finished did the tears run down her cheeks on to the pillows.

*

Rupert was welcomed back at the Barracks by his brother Officers and immediately the following morning he was sent for by Brigadier-General Bentick, the commander of the Guards Brigade.

Rupert dressed in his uniform and hurried over to his Office in the Barracks Headquarters.

"I am glad to see you back here, More," said the General, when he had entered and saluted. "I need your advice on this unholy mess we now find ourselves in."

"Is it a mess, sir?" he asked, knowing the answer.

"Of course it is, you are aware better than most that if we go to war, which now seems inevitable, we are not in as fit a state to fight as we have been in the past."

"I have always known it, sir, but I understood that nothing we asked for was done and we are obliged to carry on lacking so much indispensable ordnance."

"Exactly, More, and I have had very bad news from Turkey, and I cannot see how we can make the Army at all effective without time – time in which to put right a great number of failings that we have talked about for years, but, as you know, no one has paid the slightest attention to us."

Rupert recognised this to be true and he had heard the same refrain over and over again from his father.

In fact, as his father had eloquently pointed out, the rundown had begun just after the Battle of Waterloo.

Yet in spite of hardships and deficiencies the Army had managed to win a series of campaigns beginning with Ceylon in 1818.

Then there had been many other operations Rupert had often heard his father discuss with Senior Officers of his Regiment.

After Ceylon there had been campaigns in Burma, Northern India, China, Afghanistan and New Zealand.

Yet in 1816 the Army had been reduced to 225,000 men of whom 35,000 had formed the Army of Occupation in France.

The Duke of Wellington had personally asked that five troops of the Wagon train should be kept back to serve them, but there were then, as his father had said frequently, 35,000 men in Ireland and another 35,000 in India.

Even that was better than when three years later the Army had been reduced by a further half.

"It would help considerably, sir, if the soldiers we do have were adequately fed and equipped."

"I would agree with you, More, accommodation has always been overcrowded and in consequence unhealthy, but it is too late to do much about that now."

"Might I venture to disagree, sir?" replied Rupert. "Food is important and every Officer in this Regiment will agree with me that even here, where we are supposed to be far better off than a great many Regiments, the food is poor and monotonous."

The General stiffened.

"Are you suggesting that our men are underfed?"

"The official ration, sir, is, as you know, one pound of bread and three quarters of a pound of beef a day, but in general the soldiers are served with a beef broth of stringy meat and potatoes."

There was silence and as the General did not speak Rupert continued,

"This somewhat inadequate food is served at 7.30 am and again at 12.30 pm. There is no provision for any food between 12.30 pm and the following day. Many of the soldiers acquire extra food, particularly vegetables. In my opinion the organisation of Army catering is disgraceful."

This was certainly plain speaking and for a moment Rupert thought the General was going to tell him off.

Instead of which he muttered,

"I can see that I have been very remiss in not doing something about this situation.

"It is too late now if we go to war, but I would also like to point out, although again it is too late, that since the soldiers are wretchedly paid, most of what they do receive goes on drink.

"As you have already said, it is too late now for us to make the sort of changes required, but we must consider what we can do if, as I suspect, we are ordered abroad at any moment."

"Do you really think it is imminent, sir?"

"I am afraid so, and if we are going to be frank with each other, I should tell you that the British Army will be commanded by men who are far too old for active service."

The General was being extraordinarily frank with him which Rupert had not expected, so he enquired quietly,

"Have you been told who is to be in command?"

"The Light Division, I gather, will be commanded by Sir George Brown."

Rupert was aware that Sir George had fought with considerable distinction in the Peninsular War, but that had been forty years ago.

"Sir George de Lacy Evans will be in command of the Second Division with Sir George Cathcart, and both of them fought in the Napoleonic Wars."

"Who will command us, sir? I imagine we will be with the First Division?"

"The Duke of Cambridge and myself of course. The First Division will I am told, if we go to war, consist of one Cavalry and five Infantry Divisions."

The General spoke harshly and then as if he could not prevent himself from saying it, he added,

"All of these Divisions are under strength and lack essential transport and administrative services."

There was silence again and then Rupert remarked,

"We do have the Minié rifle, sir."

It was a new Infantry rifle and although a muzzle loader like the 'Brown Bess' it supplanted, it was a more effective weapon than had been used before.

"You are right, the Minié is an improvement, but unfortunately it is not limited to the British Army."

Rupert raised his eyebrows.

"It is not, sir?"

"No. The French have it as well, but regrettably so have the Russians."

Rupert realised this diminished the few advantages the Army had, but there was no point in saying so.

He could now only hope that the General was being unreasonably depressed and things were not quite as bad as they sounded.

There was always a reasonable chance that the Czar would abandon his ambitions and accept diplomatic defeat over Turkey – yet, as he remembered only too clearly, his father had said only a month or so ago,

"If Russia is ever to be an effective world power, it has to have the freedom not only of the Black Sea, but the Bosporus and the Dardanelles as well."

Aloud Rupert suggested,

"We can only hope and pray, sir, that it will not end in war. Surely in the meantime we should try to improve the efficiency of our own Army as quickly as possible and increase its numbers."

"That is what I hoped you would say. Therefore I want you to do everything you can to recruit more men. I also hope we can improve their living conditions."

"That is exceedingly encouraging of you, sir, and I know it will be appreciated. At the same time, as you well know, training a recruit in even the most basic elements of warfare takes time and much patience."

The General nodded as Rupert continued,

"I think you will be wise, if I may say so, to speak to the men yourself and to tell them how important it is that we should increase our numbers. So they must do all they can to encourage others to join the Army."

At first the General did not reply and then he said,

"Of course I will bring to the notice of the Higher Command the points you have just mentioned. One thing that should make us a little more cheerful about the whole matter is that I am told confidentially that the condition of the Russian Army is exceptionally bad."

"I have also heard that, but with the exception, sir, of the Cossacks who provide their own horses and arms. They therefore enjoy independence and a better standard of living than the rest of the Russian Army."

"I am sure you are right," the General agreed. "At the same time it does not make things any better where we are concerned."

"No, of course not, sir, but I can only say that, if we do go to war, all the men under my command will do their utmost because they believe we are unbeatable. They must on no account become disillusioned."

The General smiled.

"That is exactly what I expect from you, More, and I too hope that *I* will never be disillusioned."

Rupert talked with the other Officers in the Mess at luncheon time, but they left him even more depressed than he had been when with the General.

It seemed to him impossible that those in command and the politicians did not realise how utterly unprepared the Army was to engage in full scale war, especially in a part of the world they were totally unfamiliar with.

However, when it was time to dress for dinner, he was not thinking about the war any more.

He was thinking of Tania again.

*

Tania meanwhile had spent an extremely unhappy and difficult day.

She had breakfast brought up to her in the nursery and the footman who carried it up had said to her,

"Mr. Dawson thought you'd be more comfortable here, miss, than downstairs in the dining room."

Thinking that Dawson must know best, Tania had not argued but had enjoyed her breakfast.

Then she walked slowly downstairs.

She had found Dawson, as she had expected, busy in the dining room.

He was laying and decorating the large table, round which stood twenty chairs.

"Good morning, Miss Tania," he said, as she came in. "I hope you didn't mind me sending up your breakfast, but as you can see her Ladyship's ordered that there'll be twenty for luncheon and I've only just time to get it ready at such short notice."

"Twenty for luncheon! But why? And what for?"

Dawson shrugged his shoulders.

"I don't think that there be any special reason, miss, but if her Ladyship's had a good evening at one of them fancy *soirées* she goes to, she then invites a large number of people back the following day for luncheon or dinner."

"Well, I will be out for dinner, Dawson, I have been asked by some old friends of my mother's – Mr. and Mrs. Bracebridge."

"I remembers them, miss. Very kind they were to your father when he were ill. They popped in often to see him. And glad he was that they'd come."

"I am dining with them tonight, so please don't lay a place for me – "

Dawson looked uncomfortable and she asked him,

"What is wrong, Dawson?"

"Her Ladyship put on the note she writes me, that you, miss, would not be dining downstairs."

Tania drew in her breath.

She knew that this meant her stepmother intended to exclude her from all the parties she gave.

It would make things exceedingly uncomfortable if this was going to be the rule all the time she was at home.

"Am I not expected at luncheon either, Dawson?"

"I'm not certain about that, miss, you must ask Mr. Martin. He, I understands, be writing out the names of the guests to place on the table."

Tania went to the office her father's secretary had always occupied.

Mr. Martin was a man of about fifty years of age.

When she entered the office, he looked up, smiled and sprang to his feet.

"Miss Tania! It's so nice to see you again."

"It is good to see you, Mr. Martin, and I have some questions to ask you."

Tania sat down in the chair by the writing desk and he sat down too.

"What do you need to know?" he enquired.

"First whether I am expected at luncheon today."

Mr. Martin looked down at the list in front of him.

"No! Her Ladyship has put at the end, 'Miss Tania will have luncheon in the nursery'."

"And I am to be excluded from dinner too, although it happens that I am dining with friends tonight."

Mr. Martin looked embarrassed.

"I am afraid you will find things very different now you have come home, Miss Tania."

"I realise that already, but I am going first to visit Papa's Solicitors, Sinworth, Mores and Lambeth as I want to find out how much money I have of my own."

Mr. Martin smiled.

"I think you will find they are only too eager to tell you that, Miss Tania, and it is what her Ladyship has been trying to find out ever since his Lordship died."

"And has she succeeded?"

Mr. Martin shook his head.

"No, and angry and disagreeable it makes her."

He spoke to her in a low voice and glanced over his shoulder as if he was afraid of being overheard.

"Anything we say to each other, Mr. Martin, is, of coursc, private and will be repeated to no one. I must have one friend here in my own home!"

"You know I'll always be your friend, but you will understand, Miss Tania, if I offend her Ladyship, she will undoubtedly dispense with my services. As I am getting on in life, it would be hard for me to find another place where I could be as happy as I have been here."

"I understand, but I must find out if Papa has taken care of me as I am sure he has. And I cannot stay here shut away in the nursery as if I was still a child."

"I was afraid it would upset you, but her Ladyship tried everything she could to keep you at school in France."

"I know she did, but I was too old and the Mother Superior had the chance of sending me back with a num who had to return to England for family reasons. I had no choice in the matter but to come with her."

"I do understand, Miss Tania, but when your letter came and one from the Mother Superior, her Ladyship was extremely angry."

"Then you must tell me what I should do. You do understand that I cannot at my age be treated as if I was a child and there are friends of Mama's who will, I am sure, look after me if things become desperate. But I don't want to ask them unless I absolutely have to."

"You are quite right, Miss Tania, and I respect your feelings," Mr. Martin replied. "But her Ladyship is jealous in case you diminish her Social standing."

"I have no wish to do so, but I can hardly stay here day after day in the nursery. First, however, I have to find out if I have money to go anywhere else."

"I'm very sure that your father has provided for you generously, but I do think it would be a mistake for you to walk about without someone with you. Will you take one of the maids or would you like me to come with you now to the Solicitors?"

"Of course, I would like you to accompany me. If you will, it would be extremely helpful and then we must plan what I can do in the future."

She jumped up from her chair.

"I will go and fetch my hat and coat. I also want to buy some new clothes, so tell them downstairs we might not be back until late this afternoon."

He looked at her in surprise as Tania smiled at him.

"We will have luncheon together somewhere quiet, which will not shock anyone if we are seen. There must be a restaurant near here where we will not be noticed."

"Yes, of course, if it's what you want, Miss Tania, I'd be honoured," Mr. Martin managed to blurt out.

As she ran up to the nursery, Tania knew that he was surprised that she was now behaving positively like a grown-up and not a child.

'That is exactly what I am,' she told herself. 'I am no longer a young girl who just cannot move a foot without being chaperoned. And if Stepmama wants me to run my own life that is exactly what I intend to do.'

At the same time at the back of her mind she was fearful of gaining the freedom she craved.

As soon as she was ready she ran downstairs to find that Mr. Martin was waiting for her.

"I did not like to order a carriage, Miss Tania," he said, "in case her Ladyship wants it. One never knows if she'll be down when one least expects it or will stay in bed until luncheon time. We'll take a Hackney carriage."

"That will be just as convenient," Tania agreed.

However, she pondered that if her father was alive, he would have been furious at her not using his horses in the stables he was so proud of.

'I will go and see them later,' she thought, 'but first things first and my finances obviously take priority.'

It did not take them long to drive to the Solicitors in one of the streets off Piccadilly.

They knew Mr. Martin and when Tania announced who she was, she was quickly taken into the office of Mr. Sinworth.

He was the Senior Partner of the firm.

"It's such a privilege and a delight to see you, Miss Amesly," he began. "I have been worried as to when you would come home. In fact, her Ladyship told me she was not expecting you until after Christmas."

"My stepmother was anxious for me to stay abroad at school, but as you must be aware, I am too old now for school. As the Mother Superior was sending a nun back to England, she thought it would be an opportunity for me to be properly looked after on what in fact turned out to be quite an upsetting journey."

"What happened?" asked Mr. Sinworth.

Tania told him all about the train crash and how she had met two of her parent's friends on the ferry.

"I am so grateful you came to no harm," he added.

"Now I would like to know exactly what my father has left me. As you can guess, I need a great many clothes, and if I have the chance I would like to travel abroad."

She thought Mr. Sinworth raised his eyebrows.

He did not reply but merely rang a bell.

The clerk who answered it was told to bring in all the papers concerning Lord Amesly.

They were in a black tin box with Tania's father's name on the top of it.

Mr. Sinworth opened the box and brought out the will which he laid on the table.

Then he read it rather slowly while Tania listened attentively to every word.

Lord Amesly had left nine thousand pounds a year to his new wife and the house in London for her lifetime.

Everything else, including the house and estate in the country, was left to his daughter unconditionally when she reached the age of twenty-one or married.

Until then she was to be under the Guardianship of her stepmother.

"Does that mean," Tania asked Mr. Sinworth, "that she can make me do whatever she wishes, like for instance staying at school when I wanted to come home?"

"According to the law her powers are considerable, Miss Amesly, but as it will not be long before you come of age, I think it will not be very easy for her to make you do anything you do not wish to do."

Tania was not too sure, but she felt relieved.

"And money – what about money?" she asked.

"I can easily advance you anything you require at the moment within reason."

"Do you have to ask my stepmother's permission?"

There was a hesitation before Mr. Sinworth replied,

"I would not believe that if you keep within reason, there is any need to ask anyone, not even the Trustees."

"So there *are* Trustees?" Tania enquired sharply.

"Of course, of course, Miss Amesly, I am one of them as well as your uncle who lives in the North. The third Trustee is an old friend of your father's, the Earl of Grantmore."

Tania stared at him.

"Are you sure, Mr. Sinworth?"

"Very sure. When you were away your father saw a great deal of the Earl who is, I understand, now not at all well. He lives near your house in Park Lane."

He paused to make sure that Tania understood.

"When his Lordship asked him to be a Trustee, he accepted at once and said it would give him something to think about when he was immobilised and had to stay in bed."

Tania thought this an extraordinary coincidence.

But she had heard her father talk about the Earl of Grantmore. They had been at Eton and Oxford University together.

It seemed almost like fate that she should have met the Earl's son, Rupert, in such strange circumstances and was actually having dinner with him tonight!

However, she had no intention of telling any of this to Mr. Sinworth, so instead she asked him,

"I am sure you will understand that as I have been at school for so long, I do need some new clothes, in fact a whole new wardrobe. Mr. Martin and I are going shopping immediately we leave here."

Mr. Sinworth laughed.

"You are quite right. It is what any woman would do and very lovely you will look in your new clothes. Just like your dear mother, of whom I was an ardent admirer since the first day I met her."

Tania smiled.

"How much money will you give me?" she asked.

"I think the best way," Mr. Sinworth replied, "is if you send the original bills directly to me here for what you might call your '*Coming-Out Trousseau*'. I will also if you think it a bore to have to go to the bank, give Mr. Martin some money each week for you to spend casually."

Tania felt that he had a special reason for giving her money in this way and so she agreed without any fuss.

Mr. Martin was then given two hundred pounds for her as immediate cash.

"You are very kind and I am most grateful" Tania sighed.

"It is so nice to have you back, Miss Amesly, and any time you need me or are worried about anything, just come in or ask me to meet you somewhere."

Tania noticed he did not say 'at your home' and she thought he had a reason for not saying so.

She thanked him again and then she and Mr. Martin drove off in the waiting Hackney carriage.

Tania instructed the driver to take her to a shop in Bond Street, where she had often been with her mother and she recalled how delighted they had been when her mother looked so beautiful in their clothes.

Tania turned to Mr. Martin,

"Were you surprised at the way that Mr. Sinworth arranged that every bill should go to him?"

There was silence for a moment before he replied,

"I think that Mr. Sinworth was afraid her Ladyship might insist on you giving her a large amount of money. It is something she has hinted at on several occasions. Now it will be impossible for her to do so without the approval not only of Mr. Sinworth but also the other two Trustees."

Tania understood.

She was sure that her stepmother would, if it was at all possible, take every penny her father had left her.

‘She hates me,’ she thought to herself as they drove on, ‘and I will have to be so careful of everything I say and everything I do when we meet.’

The carriage drew up at the shop in Bond Street.

“Now, Mr. Martin, come and help me. As Papa’s daughter I must be the best dressed and if possible the most attractive newcomer to the Social world. We cannot afford to make any mistakes!”

Mr. Martin chuckled.

“You will do that easily, Miss Tania.”

“Nothing is ever so easy,” Tania answered, “and we must use our brains about this.”

She thought as she spoke she would really have to use her brains when it came to facing her stepmother.

Then a very different thought came into her mind.

As she went into the shop she thought that tonight she would see Rupert again, and she was determined that he, of all Selina Bracebridge’s guests, should think that she was worthy of being her father and mother’s daughter.

‘If I can only convince the Bracebridges that I am worthwhile and they love me as they loved my Mama, then I need not worry however hostile Stepmama is or however much she dislikes me in the house with her.’

As she began to look at the clothes displayed, she was thinking that tonight there would be at least one person who would be kind to her.

That was – *Rupert More.*

CHAPTER FOUR

When the Manageress realised who Tania was, she was delighted she had come to them.

"Your lady mother was one of our best customers," she trilled, "and she looked beautiful in everything she put on. Whenever she wore a new dress of ours, I had a dozen customers the next day asking if they could buy one too!"

Tania laughed.

"I am afraid I will not be as good an advertisement as that. I have just come home from school and I need an entire new wardrobe of clothes."

The Manageress took her into the fitting-room.

"If you will sit down, Miss Amesly. I will have all the new models paraded in front of you and we will choose what will suit your beauty as we chose for your mother."

Mr. Martin had said when they arrived at the shop that he would stay in the carriage.

"I have some papers to read and there is no hurry, Miss Tania. I think you will shop better without me."

Tania guessed he was feeling rather embarrassed so she replied,

"Will you forgive me for being a long time because I need so many clothes? But if I am in trouble over the accounts, I will send for you!"

Now as she sat down, the first girls came parading in front of her and she was glad she was on her own.

It made it easier to see what she wanted without asking the opinion of anyone else, least of all Mr. Martin.

Almost two hours later she came out smiling.

The Manageress was bowing to her as she stepped into the carriage.

"We are bringing two dresses with us now," Tania told Mr. Martin, "the rest are to be delivered tomorrow."

"I suppose you have bought up all the shop?"

"Practically all of it," laughed Tania. "And when I asked them to send the bill to the Solicitors, they accepted it without comment."

She felt Mr. Martin was relieved he did not have to explain anything.

When the two dress boxes were placed at the back of the carriage, she gave the footman another address.

"More shopping?" enquired Mr. Martin.

"I need some hats, I can hardly wear those I wore at school with these smart new gowns."

Mr. Martin made no comment and waited again as Tania bought half-a-dozen glamorous hats.

Next came a short pause at a shoe shop.

Tania thought she must get used to high heels, but it would be a mistake to buy too many new shoes in case they turned out to be uncomfortable.

However, she took a pair with her she intended to wear that night with a new dress when she dined with the Bracebridges.

"*Now* we can have luncheon," she proposed.

Mr. Martin gave a sigh of relief as Tania looked at her watch and gave an exclamation,

"It's very much later than I thought. Please forgive me, we should have had luncheon after the first shop."

"It is quite all right, Miss Tania, I will take you to a quiet restaurant in Shepherd's Market."

She felt guilty she had kept him waiting for so long.

Mr. Martin was well known at the small restaurant in Shepherd's Market and they were served quickly.

Tania felt too excited to be hungry.

She was longing for her new clothes to arrive and it was wonderful to be able to have the choice of a new gown every time she went out.

She had not been able to resist putting on a simple but pretty dress with a little jacket before she left the first shop and she had been even more pleased when she found a hat that matched it exactly.

"I suppose," Mr. Martin said, as they started their luncheon, "that I should have congratulated you on your new dress and hat, but I thought perhaps you would think I was being overfamiliar."

"Of course I would not think that of anything you said to me, but, as I have to live in a home where I am not welcome, I am relying on you to help me. Not only with my clothes but in everything I do and say."

Mr. Martin was silent for a minute before replying,

"I think, Miss Tania, you have to be very careful."

"In what way?"

"Where her Ladyship is concerned – "

"I am well aware of that," sighed Tania. "I am just wondering whether I should make a scene at being sent up to the nursery or whether it will be wise to say nothing and let my stepmother do the talking."

Mr. Martin hesitated.

"I think, Miss Tania, the best advice I can give you is not to quarrel with her Ladyship unless it is absolutely impossible not to."

"Why?" Tania asked him.

She knew Mr. Martin was feeling for his words and after what seemed a long moment he added,

"It is not something that I should say to you, Miss Tania, but her Ladyship is someone who always wants to have her own way and will do anything to get it."

Clearly Mr. Martin was speaking frankly and at the same time he was worried about telling her the truth.

"What you are really saying, Mr. Martin, is that her Ladyship resents my having any of Papa's money. If she could push me away, perhaps to some other sort of school, she would have more money to spend on herself."

Mr. Martin drew in his breath.

"That is something you could think, but not say – "

"I thought I was right – but I promise I will be very careful. Equally it is my home and I have nowhere else to go."

"I thought perhaps you might pay a visit to your uncle in the North? After all he is one of your Trustees."

Tania thought for a moment.

"He and Papa never got on very well and he never made any effort to see me or communicate with me."

"Perhaps there are some other relatives?"

"If there are I don't know about them. Mama was adored by all her own family, but they were all older than her and I think there are very few, if any, of them left."

Mr. Martin sighed.

"You will have to see exactly what her Ladyship is planning for you, Miss Tania, and of course I will help you whenever I can. But you do realise it is difficult for me."

She could understand he did not wish to take sides.

"Perhaps things will be better than we both fear. I am fortunate in having made friends with two people who loved Mama and who are being very kind to me already."

"I think that if you look around you will find a lot of people who remember your mother and father – but they are not being so friendly to her Ladyship."

When they had finished luncheon, Mr. Martin said they must return to the house.

"I did not expect to be away quite so long and if her Ladyship has sent for me, she will be annoyed to find that I am not in the house."

Tania reckoned from the way he spoke that he was really frightened of offending her stepmother.

So she hurried out to the carriage and Mr. Martin joined her as soon as he had paid the bill.

As he climbed into the carriage, he suggested,

"I had better give you the money that the Solicitor gave me. It would be better for it to be in your keeping than in mine."

Tania said nothing as she thought that he was really implying that her stepmother, if she realised he had been given two hundred pounds for her, would undoubtedly find some reason for snatching it away for her own pocket.

Tania took the money from him and then they told the driver to take them back to Park Lane.

Tania was thinking that after her stepmother's large luncheon party the guests should have left by this time.

However, when they arrived at Amesly House there were still two carriages waiting outside.

Their driver therefore stopped outside in the street and she and Mr. Martin climbed out.

"I expect they will be in the drawing room," Tania commented, "so I will go straight upstairs."

She told the footman to take the two dress boxes up to the nursery.

She reached the front door and Dawson opened it for her and as she stepped into the house, Tania was aware that her stepmother was standing in the middle of the hall.

She was saying goodbye to a middle-aged man and as she entered, Lady Amesly gave a cry and exclaimed,

"Tania! And where have you been? You have no right to go out without telling me where you were going."

"I understood, Stepmama, that you were asleep and I did not think you would want me to wake you."

The man standing beside Lady Amesly laughed.

"That's a perfectly good excuse, Isobel, and there is no point in your saying otherwise."

"I can see that you have been out shopping, Tania," Lady Amesly snarled.

"I certainly needed some new clothes."

"Suppose you introduce me," the departing guest suggested. "The only thing I do know about clothes is that they are very expensive!"

Tania laughed.

"That is true! I needed new clothes badly and it has taken me a long and exhausting time to buy them. That is why I am late."

"If what you are wearing is part of what you have been buying," said the man, "then I congratulate you, and it is only right for me to tell you that you look entrancing."

Tania laughed again.

"That is exactly what I like to hear and it makes me feel that I have not spent money to no purpose."

"I should hope not indeed!" huffed Lady Amesly.

She turned towards the man.

"Goodbye, Roger. As you realise, I have to see to my stepdaughter. She has just arrived back from France where she has been at school."

"Well, one lesson they taught her," the man called Roger answered, "is how to dress herself with a Parisian *chic* which I am sure will delight every man in London."

He put out his hand towards Tania,

"Goodbye, Tania, and allow me to congratulate you on your excellent taste. I will look forward to meeting you again, I hope very shortly."

Tania put her hand in his.

As she did so, she thought, although it was strange, that this man was not a particularly nice person.

She could hardly explain it to herself, but there was something about him, which, despite the pleasant words he was mouthing, she felt was repulsive and creepy.

Then releasing her hand and turning towards her stepmother, he said,

"Goodbye, Isobel, and thank you for the delightful luncheon. I will see you this evening at eight o'clock and I promise not to be late."

"If you are, I would worry that you have forgotten me," Lady Amesly responded in what Tania thought was a somewhat seductive voice.

"That would be impossible," he answered lightly.

Taking his hat from one of the footmen, he walked out of the front door.

Lady Amesly walked towards the drawing room.

"Come with me, Tania," she demanded sharply, "I wish to talk to you."

There was nothing Tania could do but follow her.

She realised that Mr. Martin had vanished almost as if he had been a ghost.

They entered the drawing room and Lady Amesly closed the door.

"*Just how dare you,*" she began furiously, "go out shopping without my permission?"

"I needed some new clothes very badly and I went first to see the Solicitors."

"Solicitors! Why should you go to see them?"

"Because Papa sent me a letter when he became so ill saying that if anything happened to him, the Solicitors would explain everything to me. I therefore did exactly as he wanted me to do."

"That is for me to say, Tania, and I presume from the way that you are now dressed that is what you have been spending *my* money on."

"No! I only spent money that Papa left me and the bills have all gone to the Solicitors."

Lady Amesly glared at her.

"What are you saying? Why should the Solicitors pay your bills?"

"Because they thought it was the best way of doing things. I wish to spend a considerable amount of money on clothes. You must be aware that I have not had anything new for the last two years."

"I have never heard such impertinence in my life," Lady Amesley erupted. "*I* am your Guardian and you will have to do as I tell you and not take things upon yourself in this monstrous manner."

"I had no wish to trouble you," said Tania calmly, "and I cannot believe you wish me to go on wearing, now I have returned to London, the clothes I wore at school. Not one has been replaced as the Mother Superior expected me to leave sooner than I was able to do."

"It is exceedingly irritating," Lady Amesly sneered after a short pause, "that the Mother Superior would not keep you as I wished her to do."

"I am too old – too old to be at school. Now I am back, I am hoping I will have the chance to enjoy myself as Mama and Papa would have wished me to do."

"I think that's very unlikely, Tania, as I find young girls a bore and so do the friends I am entertaining tonight. You will therefore take your dinner upstairs as you should have had your luncheon."

"Actually, as it so happens, I am going out tonight. I have been invited to dinner by two of Mama's friends."

"Friends! What friends?"

"Mr. and Mrs. Bracebridge, who live in Belgrave Square."

She saw by the expression on her stepmother's face that she knew who they were and she had doubtless wanted to be friends with them.

Her next question proved this supposition.

"Did they ask *me*?"

"No. They asked me because we travelled together on the ferry and they decided that they would give a dinner party for me to meet some of my parents' close friends."

For a moment Lady Amesly did not have anything to say, so Tania added,

"So you see I should not be intruding on your party, and it is extremely nice for me to meet so soon those who loved Papa and Mama."

Lady Amesly was silent for a moment and then she spoke up,

"When you visited the Solicitors, they undoubtedly told you what your father left you in his will. I hope you realise that keeping up this house and the country estate is expensive and I expect you to contribute generously to the trouble I have taken whilst you have been abroad."

"I would, of course, have to ask my Solicitors and doubtless my Trustees about that suggestion."

"Why would you ask them?"

"It was the arrangement Papa made before he died, and I am only too happy to carry out his wishes."

She felt there would be no answer to this assertion and so she walked towards the door.

"Forgive me, Stepmama, but I must go upstairs and unpack the items I have bought. I want to wear one of my new dresses this evening."

She reached the door as she finished speaking.

Then before her stepmother could think of what to say next, Tania had left the drawing room.

She hurried upstairs to find that the two dress boxes had been handed to her maid.

"Do you wish me to hang these up now, miss?" she asked as Tania entered the nursery.

"Yes, Betsy, and I will wear the prettiest tonight."

She was thinking as she took off her hat and jacket that she had escaped rather lightly from her stepmother.

She had almost forgotten while she was away how much she resented her and how disagreeable she could be if she did not have her own way.

She certainly now looked much older and Tania felt that she had grown even nastier than she remembered her being during the last holidays she had spent in England.

Her stepmother had clearly been extremely jealous of every kind word and thought her father had for her, and she had done everything in her power to make him see her as a tiresome troublesome child.

And if she had been jealous of her then, Tania was certain she would be even more jealous of her now.

Especially when she was well dressed and too old to be punished as she had tried to punish her before she had gone away to school.

At the same time, judging by the fact she had been pushed up into the nursery, it was going to be a hard battle and Tania wished with all her heart and soul that there was somewhere else she could live.

Then she told herself that she would not allow her stepmother to spoil this evening.

She would be dining with a couple who were kind and loving and of course with Rupert –

It was then she remembered he said that he would call on her at six o'clock.

She wondered how she could manage to talk to him without her stepmother interfering and perhaps even being offensive to her in front of him.

She was still wondering what she could do when Betsy came out of the bedroom.

"I've hung 'em up, miss, and I thinks there be some more parcels arrivin' tomorrow. Mr. Martin has told me to look out for them."

"Yes, I hope there will be, Betsy. The shoes which go with the dress I am going to wear were in the Hackney carriage. The footman should have brought them up with the other boxes."

"I'll go and find them, miss. A letter comes for you while you was out. It be on the table."

Tania had not looked at the nursery table and now she saw a letter addressed to her.

She knew even before she opened it, who it must be from and she thought perhaps Rupert was telling her that he would not be able to come to the party tonight.

It was with a sense of relief that she read,

"*My dear Tania,*

Owing to unforeseen orders I cannot, alas, join you as I wanted to do, at six o'clock.

However, I have ordered my father's carriage to take us to the party in Belgrave Square and I will call for you at about seven-thirty.

Please you must forgive me for not keeping my first engagement, but you will understand just why when I tell you what is happening."

It was signed simply,

"*Yours sincerely, Rupert.*"

He had strong upright writing and Tania thought it was exactly how, looking as he did, he ought to write.

She was sorry he could not come to see her, but it would save her the difficulty of explaining why she was in the nursery and could not receive him in the drawing room.

*

The fact was that Rupert had been sent for by the Secretary of State for War.

Sir Sidney Herbert, who had been a Minister in Sir Robert Peel's Government, had now been given the most impossible task it was possible to imagine.

He had only just been appointed Secretary for War by the Prime Minister.

Half-brother to the Earl of Pembroke and heir to the famous Wilton House in Wiltshire, Sir Sidney was one of the most popular and admired men in London.

He was good-looking, had great intelligence and a genuine love for his fellow men. He was an excellent shot and a bold rider to hounds.

He was exceedingly rich and a devout Christian and his Parliamentary career had been outstanding.

Rupert was welcomed at the War Office and taken immediately into Sir Sidney's office.

He rose when Rupert entered and held out his hand.

"I asked to see you, More," he began, "because you may know that the current situation is extremely bad and deteriorating."

"I have only just returned to England, Sir Sidney, and I am therefore not fully up-to-date with events, but the newspapers are all full of gloom."

Sir Sidney sighed.

"Yes, it is indeed much worse than we anticipated and I am almost certain that our diplomats will not be as astute as we hoped they would be."

"You definitely think it will be war, Sir Sidney?"

Rupert was a great admirer of Sidney Herbert and he knew it was unlikely that he would be clever enough to achieve peace when everyone else was becoming more or less resigned to war.

Rupert was only too well aware, as perhaps another man might not have been, of the difficulties the Secretary for War was already encountering.

The Prime Minister, Lord Aberdeen, was a man of great integrity, but he was inclined to believe what he was told by people who wanted to please him.

The Home Secretary, Lord Palmerston, held a view that was totally opposite to that of the Prime Minister.

There was, Rupert felt, a great conflict of opinion in the Cabinet and it was almost impossible for the British to exert much influence in the worsening situation between the Czar and the Sultan of Turkey.

He had been told by a friend last night after he had arrived that the Russians believed the British were going through a phase of pacifism and they were sure the British were unlikely to intervene in anything they did.

It was no use Rupert telling his friend this was not the case as he knew that the Czar felt passionately that he had good reason to go ahead and declare war on Turkey.

Sir Sidney Herbert asked Rupert to sit down.

"I want you to organise the recruitment of as many men as you can, More, and start training them at once."

"You really think there will be war?" asked Rupert.

"I should be lying if I said to you I was optimistic," replied Sir Sidney.

They then attempted to think how they could do the impossible – which was to enlist and train a great number of troops before war was actually declared.

Once again Rupert put forward his ideas for better food for the Army and a more comfortable life in Barracks as he had to his General.

He was pleased to find that Sir Sidney agreed with everything he said and yet they were both aware that it would be impossible to achieve what he was asking for in a very short time frame.

However, as Rupert left the War Office Sir Sidney confided in him,

"One thing we both must do is to keep smiling and make sure there is no panic amongst our own people.

"I think the war will be too far away for the British to realise just how terrible it will be if it does take place. Anyway let's you and me forget it for tonight."

Rupert looked at him questioningly.

"*Tonight*, Sir Sidney?"

It did flash through his mind that perhaps he was expected to go to some Regimental or Official dinner.

In which case he would not see Tania.

"I understand you are dining with the Bracebridges, as I am," Sir Sidney replied. "I saw Charles this morning and he told me what trouble you had experienced in a train crash in France and that you rescued the beautiful daughter of an old friend of your father's."

Rupert thought that Charles Bracebridge must have been rather too voluble on the subject, but he merely said,

"I am so glad you are coming to the party tonight, Sir Sidney, and I am certain you will think Miss Amesly worth saving!"

The Secretary for War laughed.

*

Rupert hurried off to change his clothes for dinner.

He had first to see his father who was still in bed, but reading the newspapers.

"I suppose these damn fools are going to involve us in another war," he fumed as his son entered the room.

"I am afraid so, Papa."

"Did I not tell you that this would all happen if we went on neglecting the Army and allowed it to wither away to nothing? Heavens above! Why should we be governed by one idiotic Prime Minister after another who can never see further than the end of his nose?"

Rupert had heard all this before, so he sat down at his father's bedside.

"Papa you should be coming to the party I told you about tonight. And apparently Sir Sidney Herbert is an old friend of the Bracebridges."

"I know and you can tell him from me that it is too late now to blame the idiots who have preceded him. If he can produce an effective Army at a moment's notice out of the ground, he is a magician and there's no other word for it."

Rupert sighed.

"I do agree with you, Papa. But there is nothing we can do but recruit as many men as possible. I am supposed to train them before we leave."

"Those politicians are damn fools!" his father said furiously. "If I were well enough, I would go to the House of Lords and say so."

"It is too late. Even if they listened to you, there would be nothing they could suggest beyond what we are now trying to do. And you are right, it needs a miracle to produce trained soldiers out of nowhere."

"Of course it's impossible, my boy, and by the way, what's the name of the young girl you were telling me you rescued from the train?"

"Tania Amesly. And I understand you knew her father. In fact, you are one of her Trustees."

"Good Lord, so I am! I thought I recognised that name – I am getting senile. If you ask me it is this damned treatment the doctors are giving me!

"It is not that my brain does not work, it is because they fill it full of rubbish, which makes me feel as if I am walking through a fog all the time."

"Then don't take it, Papa, I'm sure it is a mistake to take too many doctors' medicines. Because they think you are so rich and can afford to pay them, they pop in and out simply to gorge money out of you."

"I have never heard a truer word. I will throw away my doctor's medicines and rely on the herbs your mother grew in the Herb Garden in the country."

"I honestly think, Papa, you would feel better if you followed her advice. They used to call her a 'white witch' in the village. It was only after she healed them that they altered the second word to '*angel*'."

The Earl smiled.

"You are quite right, my boy, as always. I will now give up all these pills and go to the country. The servants there knew that what your mother made for the villagers worked and that is the medicine I shall take in the future."

"I'm sure you would feel better, Papa, and if I have to go overseas, which seems inevitable, I would be much happier if I thought you were being looked after at home."

"You are right, Rupert, but I will stay here until you actually go. Otherwise I will never see you."

"I will see as much of you as I possibly can, Papa, but it looks as if I will be kept very busy."

He was thinking as he dressed for dinner that he wanted to see not only his father but Tania as well.

He had never imagined that any woman could be such fun as she had been at sea. She had enjoyed as he had the waves rocking the ship and splashing over the decks.

'I have never met anyone like her,' he mused again.

Later, when he was told that his carriage was at the door, he hurriedly went to say goodnight to his father who was half asleep.

Then he ran down the steps and told the coachman to take him first to Amesly House.

"I knows where it be, sir," called the coachman.

Rupert then jumped in, feeling a strange excitement of anticipation that he had not felt for a long time.

*

Tania was feeling exactly the same.

She was so relieved she would not have to endure yet another uncomfortable encounter with her stepmother before she left.

She had no wish for her to see the very beautiful evening gown she was wearing

Actually it had indeed cost what she thought was an extravagant amount of money, but it was so attractive she had felt she must put it on for the party tonight.

Tania had good taste that she had inherited from her mother.

The gown highlighted her figure and enhanced her own unique aura.

It gave her in some way almost a spiritual look and yet when she was laughing she was the personification of youth and happiness.

She had fortunately found a lovely cape that would go with all her gowns and would keep her warm when the night was cool.

When she had finished dressing, Betsy exclaimed with delight,

"You really looks lovely, miss, and there won't be a gentleman at the party who won't tell you so!"

"I hope you are right, Betsy, but I expect I will have a lot of competition."

She was musing that if the Bracebridges were going to ask her mother's friends to dinner, most of them would be older than her.

Going to the door, she opened it and listened.

She could hear her stepmother's guests arriving and she knew that she would be in the drawing room waiting to receive them.

When there was a short pause between arrivals, she hurried down the stairs.

Dawson was in the hall and she whispered to him,

"I will be in the morning room, Dawson. When I see the carriage coming for me, I will come out quickly."

She did not need to explain the reason that she had no wish to see her stepmother or for her stepmother to see her.

Dawson understood perfectly,

"Please don't worry, Miss Tania. If the gentleman asks for you, I'll see that the drawing room door is closed afore you comes out of the morning room."

Tania smiled at him.

"Thank you, Dawson. I don't want any trouble just before I go out for dinner."

"Of course not, Miss Tania. You leave it to me."

It was just three minutes after half-past seven when Tania, gazing out of the window of the morning room, saw a carriage draw up outside the front door.

Before the footman could climb down from the box the man inside let himself out.

It was Rupert.

Tania felt a sudden leap of her heart as she ran to the door.

As she opened it she heard Rupert's deep voice say,

"I am calling for Miss Amesly."

"She's ready waiting for you, sir," replied Dawson.

Tania, pulling her cloak around her, stepped out of the morning room.

She ran across the hall and down the steps.

Rupert helped her into the carriage.

Even as they drove off another carriage came up behind them and Tania guessed that it was another of her stepmother's friends arriving.

She smiled at Rupert and he commented,

"I have a feeling you have escaped rather than just left!"

"My stepmother is having a party tonight," Tania answered demurely, "and I don't want to be involved with her guests."

"You are looking *so* lovely," Rupert sighed, "and I wish I was taking you out alone rather than having to go to a party."

Tania smiled.

"I am sure that is something I would not be allowed to do."

"But perhaps we can before I do go away?"

She looked at him her eyes opening apprehensively.

"*Go away*!" she exclaimed, "do you mean to war?"

"The reason I could not meet you earlier is because I had to see the Secretary for War and I am afraid war is inevitable, Tania, and before we go I'm afraid that I will be very busy. So it is unlikely I will be able to see as much of you as I would wish."

Tania drew in her breath.

"I want to see you too," she murmured.

They were passing a lighted lamp as she spoke and Rupert thought her large eyes looking up into his was the most beautiful sight he had ever seen.

"I met you by chance, Tania, and I am determined not to lose you now."

Tania had a strange feeling within her breast.

It felt as if her heart was beating unrestrainedly.

"I feel just the same, Rupert, it was such fun when we were on the ferry."

"I think it will always be fun when we are together, but war is war, and as you know I am a soldier."

"You must take very great care of yourself."

Rupert smiled at her and she knew, although he did not reply, he was thinking that was impossible in the face of the enemy.

She tried to think of something she could say.

Something which would make him realise that she wanted him to come back to her.

Then the horses drew up outside the Bracebridge's house in Belgrave Square.

There were flares blazing outside the door and two carriages were moving away ahead of them.

"It looks as if it is going to be a big party," Tania muttered.

"All in your honour, Tania, you should be flattered. I am told that the parties given by the Bracebridges are always much sought after and extremely enjoyable."

"Just as I was so lucky when you found me on the train, so I am lucky now we have come back to London."

"Then let us hope our luck will never fail," Rupert added as a footman opened the door of the carriage.

CHAPTER FIVE

The house in Belgrave Square was, as Tania had expected, large, well furnished and extremely impressive.

She was welcomed most affectionately by Selina Bracebridge and her husband and they were also delighted to see Rupert.

"I am afraid that you have come home to very bad news," Charles said to Rupert.

"You are right, it is extremely bad," agreed Rupert.

"We are expecting Sidney Herbert later," Charles went on, "so he will undoubtedly tell us the worst."

Then other guests were announced and Tania and Rupert moved away.

Fortunately he knew many people in the room and as their host and hostess were busy, he introduced Tania to his friends.

They were a party of eighteen for dinner and Tania found herself sitting, not beside Rupert as she had hoped, but between two pleasant young men who paid her many compliments and made her laugh.

They certainly added considerably to the bright and amusing atmosphere of the occasion.

It was only after dinner was over that a number of older guests arrived and then Tania realised that Selina had been kind enough to invite only the young for dinner.

They congregated in the drawing room and Tania

found so many of them spoke of her mother and father with affection that she felt tears coming into her eyes.

"Your mother was the most beautiful person I have ever seen," one lady told her, "and your father was indeed one of the most popular men in the whole Social world."

It was exactly what Tania wanted to hear and it was marvellous to feel that her parents had not been forgotten.

They did not dance, but Selina promised that there would be a dance another night, so the younger guests left early and then the older ones, who had either been talking or playing card games, thought it was time to leave too.

When Tania and Rupert were about to depart, the big reception room was almost empty.

"You must come and see me if you feel lonely or are missing your mother," Selina told Tania. "Just run in and if I am not here, wait until I come back."

"You are so kind and as I am not welcome at home, I am afraid you may find me dropping in at any moment!"

"That is just what I want you to do, Tania. Charles and I will be very pleased to see Rupert as well."

"I only hope I am able to accept your invitation," said Rupert. "But as you know, things seem very worrying at present."

As he was speaking the door opened and the butler announced,

"Sir Sidney Herbert, ma'am."

He strode into the room as Selina held out her arms.

"Oh, Sidney, I am so very pleased to see you. I was afraid, as you didn't come earlier, you could not get away."

"I only managed it at the last moment," Sir Sidney responded, "and I had no wish to disappoint you and not to hear about your adventures in Germany."

Then he saw Rupert and beckoned him over,

"I would like a word with you, More."

"I was just leaving, Sir Sidney – "

"Then please wait for just a moment."

Rupert hurried towards him and then they walked to the far end of the room and stood by the window.

Sir Sidney was obviously telling Rupert something that was too important to be overheard by anyone else.

Tania waited a little uncomfortably.

She was afraid that Rupert might not be able to take her back home as she so hoped.

Then leaving Sir Sidney he came across to her and she realised with relief that the conversation was over and they could now leave.

They said farewell to the Bracebridges and thanked them both for a wonderful evening.

"Come in tomorrow if you have time," Selina said to Tania. "I have some engagements, but I will be here at teatime."

"I would love to, Mrs. Bracebridge, and thank you again a thousand times."

At the front door Rupert's carriage was waiting for them.

He gave the coachman his instructions after she had stepped in, so that she did not hear what he said.

Then as Rupert joined her, she felt that there was something wrong as he did not speak.

"What is it? What has happened?" she enquired.

"It is as I feared, Tania, the British Government is declaring war on Russia tomorrow!"

Tania gave a cry.

"So what has happened?"

"As you may not know, the Foreign Secretary sent a sharp note after the Russians had sunk a Turkish Naval Squadron in the Black Sea, stating that unless they agreed to evacuate the two countries of Moldavia and Wallachia by April there would be war."

Tania was listening to him intently, but she could not fully understand all that Rupert was telling her.

He continued,

"The Russians, however, have not waited and have already said that they have no intention of complying. *In consequence we and France have declared war*."

"How can we possibly fight them, Rupert, when as you said we are not ready and don't have enough troops?"

"We can only hope that with the help of France we will be able to give Russia the lesson they richly deserve."

"Then it means you have to go, Rupert?"

"Yes, I must, and our troops are not really ready for such an expedition. But it has to be done and that means I will have to leave – you."

The way he spoke made Tania turn to look at him.

In the darkness of the carriage with the only light coming from the lamps they passed, it was difficult to see the expression on his face.

Yet she knew instinctively that his vibrations were reaching out to touch hers.

"You must take great care of yourself, Rupert," she whispered softly.

"I will take care because I really want to return to you. We have only just met, Tania, but I knew as soon as I saw you that you would mean a great deal in my life and that you are so different from anyone else."

"Do you really feel like that?" she asked. "I think I feel the same about *you* – "

He smiled.

"That makes things very easy, but I am not going to ask you to make any quick decision about our future."

Tania drew in her breath.

"It would be most unfair and unjust to you, when I am going away for Heaven knows how long, to make you feel yourself tied to me. If and when I return, I will say what I am longing to say to you now."

"Will it really be a long time?" Tania asked him in a soft hesitating little voice.

"You know exactly what I am feeling and therefore, my darling, because *I love you*, I am going to say nothing more until, please God, I return."

Tania gasped.

She wanted to say a thousand things to him and beg him to tell her what he meant by saying he loved her.

But she realised he was keeping an iron control on himself and she must let him do things his way – not hers.

"I am going to ask you just one question," Rupert murmured after what seemed a long silence.

"What is it?" Tania asked breathlessly

"What do you feel about me? Just tell me the truth."

There was a pause and then Tania whispered,

"I think I love you, but I am so ignorant about love. I only know that I want to be with you for always. I would have found this evening dull and empty if you had not been there."

"Oh, my sweet darling Tania, that is the beginning of love and there are a thousand things I can teach you later about love. Love is something I have always dreamt about, but thought would never happen to me in real life."

"I dreamt that you would find me, Rupert."

"I dreamt I would find someone perfect. Someone who would love me not for my family, nor my money, not for anything except the love which makes two people one, and enables them to be supremely happy not just for a few years but for ever."

"That is what I want too. As I have said, I know so little about love. I have met hardly any men having only just left school, but I have always believed that one day, like my Papa and Mama, I would find a person who would make me so happy that nothing else in the world mattered."

"That is exactly what we will find together, Tania, but I must, my darling one, leave you free, in case we are mistaken and you find someone else whom you love more than you love me."

"I am absolutely certain that will never happen and I will think of you, Rupert, and pray for you every day you are away."

"God knows I will need your prayers, but I do feel they will give me an invisible armour that will enable me to come back to you."

As he spoke he picked up her hand.

At his touch she felt herself tremble with a strange excitement.

"How can you possibly be so beautiful?" he asked. "As a thousand men will tell you when I am not here."

"If they do, I will merely wish it was *you* telling me and not them."

Almost with a cry she asked,

"When will I see you again, Rupert?"

"I would hope and pray that I will be able to see you tomorrow. But after what Sidney Herbert told me this evening, I know we will have to move to the coast where there are ships waiting to take us to the Black Sea."

"Tomorrow! But how can you possibly, possibly be ready by then?"

"It seems an impossibility at present, but we have already foreseen this and therefore most of our equipment has been packed and has only to be moved to the coast.

"It will take us a long time, perhaps over a month, to actually reach Varna on the Black sea. Of course by that time the Russians may have taken up their positions, so we are not at all certain where we will finally land."

"It sounds terribly muddling and I cannot imagine why you have to go to a war that seems to be almost at the other end of the world," Tania sighed.

Rupert smiled.

"That is the right way to put it, but we have, I think, to be as mobile as possible and not make rigid plans which cannot be adjusted to the circumstances."

He made a gesture with his hands as he added,

"No one appears to know what is happening, except that the Russians are being horribly cruel to their Turkish prisoners of war, who fought gallantly to no avail."

"I am frightened for you," murmured Tania. "Very very frightened."

"I have to do what is right, Tania. It is after all what I have trained for and worked towards for many years. It is only because at this last moment I have found you that I so wish I could stay in England longer and tell you again and again how beautiful you are and how much I love you."

As he spoke the carriage came to a standstill.

Tania realised that having driven round Hyde Park while they had been talking, they had now stopped outside her house in Park Lane.

The coachman opened the door.

Tania then turned to Rupert feeling tearful.

"You really cannot leave me like this. I *must* say goodbye to you."

Rupert did not reply and as she climbed out of the carriage, the front door was opened by the night footman.

Rupert turned to his coachman,

"Wait for me, Wilkins, I will not be long."

The coachman raised his hand to his hat and Rupert walked into the house beside Tania.

There were only a few lights left on in the hall and they made for the drawing room.

For a second Tania was afraid that her stepmother's guests had not left and she would be still there.

Even as the thought flashed through her mind, she was aware that, if there was only one footman in the hall, it meant the party was over and Dawson had gone to bed.

They went into the drawing room and then Rupert closed the door.

They were in complete darkness with the exception of the moonlight coming in through one window where the curtain must have been left undrawn by mistake.

It was letting in a silver light that touched the floor.

For a moment they stood close to each other.

Then slowly, as if he had no wish to frighten her, or to spoil the magic that was enveloping them both, Rupert drew Tania close into his arms.

"I love you, Tania" he breathed. "Try to remember me, and, as you said, pray for me every day. I will dream of you every single night I am away – "

Then he was kissing her.

Kissing her at first gently as if not to frighten her.

He felt her body melting into his and then her lips became responsive as his kisses became more possessive.

He kissed her and went on kissing her.

Tania felt as if they were part of the moonlight and he was carrying her up into the sky and they were dancing amongst the stars.

Then without another word he released her, opened the door and hurried out into the hall.

He closed the door behind him leaving her standing in the drawing room.

She heard his footsteps until there was the sound of the front door closing behind him.

It was then that she put her hands up to her face.

It was impossible for her to believe what had just happened – but now Rupert had gone.

'I love him, I adore him,' she whispered into the moonlight.

The strange sensations that had moved in her body, that she was unable to express in words, had changed her whole being.

It was a long time later before she left the drawing room and climbed slowly upstairs to the nursery.

The lights had been left on for her, but she did not see any of her childhood toys, only Rupert's face.

When she climbed into bed and was once again in the darkness, she could still feel his lips on hers.

Her unbelievable intense feelings she now realised was ecstasy were still sweeping through her body.

'I love Rupert, of course, I love him,' she said over and over again to herself.

It seemed unthinkable that he had come and gone just like that.

Yet she knew it was he and only he who now filled her life.

Nothing and nobody else was of any significance.

She thought it would be impossible to sleep.

But actually she did fall asleep and dreamt she was still in Rupert's arms and he was kissing her endlessly.

*

When she woke with a start she was aware it was later than usual.

She then guessed that Betsy must have come into the room and seeing her asleep had crept away.

Tania realised that this was so when she found on opening her bedroom door that her breakfast was waiting for her in the nursery.

Because she knew it would get cold, she put on her dressing gown to eat it at once.

Only when she had finished her breakfast and was practically dressed, a footman came up to the nursery.

"Good morning, Henry," said Tania.

"Mornin', miss," the footman replied. "These here flowers has just arrived for you and there be a letter too."

Tania gave an exclamation of excitement.

When she took the flowers from the footman, she saw that they were white lilies and white roses.

She just knew that they were from Rupert.

The footman left her and she sat down in a chair to open the letter.

It was very short and yet it told her everything she wanted to know.

Rupert had written,

"*My darling precious one,*

"*I love you, I do love you, Tania. Think of me and pray for me as you promised you would.*

Remember that wherever I am I will be with you – always and forever.

Rupert."

It was not only her first love letter but a letter from the man she loved and she would always treasure it.

It was more important than anything she could ever own.

Very gently she kissed the letter before she put it back into its envelope and then she looked at the flowers.

She felt as if Rupert was standing there beside her, telling her that to him she was as pure as the lilies and as beautiful as the white roses.

She arranged them in a vase and put them on the nursery table.

She stood looking at them, thinking of Rupert and wondering where he was at this very moment.

As she did so Betsy came in.

"Her Ladyship wants to speak to you, Miss Tania," she said, "and her be in the boudoir next to her bedroom."

Because it was the room her mother had always used, Tania wished she could refuse to go.

Then she told herself it was of no matter and that if Rupert was brave enough to confront the enemy, she could confront *hers*.

As she finished dressing she found herself wishing that he could see her in the dress she had bought yesterday.

Then she walked slowly down the stairs.

When she entered the boudoir, her stepmother was sitting at the writing table.

"So good morning to you, Tania," she began in an unexpectedly pleasant tone. "I wished to speak to you, but as you came in so late, I learnt you were not available until now."

"I was rather late," admitted Tania.

"I do hope you enjoyed your party," her stepmother added amicably.

Tania was surprised but answered politely,

"It was a most enjoyable evening and Mr. and Mrs. Bracebridge were extremely kind to me."

"And now I am going to be even kinder to you. Sit down, Tania, and listen to what I have to say to you."

Tania sat down obediently on a chair by the desk.

When she took a good look at her stepmother, she had to admit that she was good-looking, in fact *very* good-looking for her age and she could understand in a way why her father had married her.

"I have been thinking about your position now you have come home, and I have decided that as you are older than most of the girls who have just left school, it would be wise for you to be married as soon as possible."

"*Married!*" ejaculated Tania. "What do you mean?"

"Exactly what I say and I have in fact just found the ideal husband for you."

For a moment Tania was speechless.

She could not believe what she was hearing.

"The gentleman you met here yesterday was Lord Watford, who is very anxious to marry and have an heir. His first wife died giving birth to a stillborn child. He is lonely and he is also very rich."

She looked at Tania sternly as she carried on,

"As soon as he saw you, he decided that you were exactly the wife he had been looking for and he is coming here today to tell you so."

Tania was listening wide-eyed.

She had difficulty in finding the right words to say, but finally she exploded,

"*You must be mad*! I will not marry a man I have barely met and whom I do not love. It so happens that for the moment I don't wish to marry anyone."

As she spoke she told herself that what she felt for Rupert and he felt for her must stay a secret between them. Her love for Rupert was very precious to her and certainly could never be discussed or spoilt by her stepmother.

"I think you are forgetting one very simple point," Lady Amesly countered frostily.

"What is that?"

"As you were told yesterday by the Solicitors, and which was confirmed to me this morning by Mr. Martin, I am your Guardian until you reach the age of twenty-one or are married. Therefore you have to obey me."

"Not about something as important as marrying a man I do not love and who cannot possibly love me."

Lady Amesly laughed unpleasantly.

"Really you cannot be so naïve as not to realise you are very pretty and have every qualification that someone like Lord Watford requires."

She paused and as Tania was incapable of speaking, she went on,

"You come from an aristocratic family, you have your own money and he finds you attractive. You are truly a most fortunate girl in being offered marriage by such a charming and distinguished gentleman."

"But I refuse! I totally refuse to marry anyone I do not love," Tania persisted.

Her stepmother's eyes narrowed.

"As I have already pointed out, you have to do as I tell you. I will see that you are married to Roger Watford if I have to *drag* you to the altar. You stupid, idiotic girl! You should be down on your knees thanking God that you have the chance of marrying someone of distinction who will give you a good position in Society."

"He is too old! He is old enough to be my father. Anyway even if he really was the most important man in the world, I could never marry him unless I loved him."

"You will do as I tell you, Tania! Otherwise I will have you taken off to an asylum for women who, if they are not completely mad, are in no way capable of looking after themselves."

"*You cannot do that to me!*" Tania yelled furiously.

"It is impossible for you to stop me, as I am your appointed Guardian, from doing anything I think is right and proper for you."

Tania gave a strangled cry.

Then as if she could not bear to hear any more, she jumped up from the chair and ran out of the room.

As she slammed the door behind her, she heard her stepmother laughing.

She realised that it was the sound of a woman who was quite certain her plans could not be refused or altered.

'How can she do this to me? How is it possible?' Tania asked herself feverishly.

She ran up to the nursery, collected Rupert's letter, her hat, her handbag and as an afterthought the money Mr. Martin had given her and then ran down the stairs again.

As she neared the hall, she hesitated just in case her stepmother was there and if she was, she would doubtless prevent her leaving the house.

To her relief there was only one of the footmen and without any question, he opened the door for her when she signalled him to do so.

She stepped into Park Lane.

Then to her relief a Hackney carriage was coming slowly down the road and when she waved, it stopped.

She jumped in and gave the driver the address of the Bracebridge's house in Belgrave Square.

And as he whipped up his horse, she glanced back at the house in case her stepmother was running after her.

To her relief the door was closed and she guessed that it had not yet occurred to Lady Amesly that she might run away.

And now she could only hope frantically that the Bracebridges would help her.

She was desperately afraid they might not wish to be involved in what was purely a family row.

'If only I could ask Rupert, he would know what to do,' she thought.

It flashed through her mind that perhaps, after all he had said, he would marry her before he left the country.

But she knew that because she loved him, she could not give him the extra strain of leaving a wife behind.

'I love him. I adore him,' she told herself over and over. 'But he has enough worries at the moment, keeping himself and his men alive and I must not add to them.'

It did not take the Hackney carriage long to reach Belgrave Square.

She then paid off the driver, thinking that if Selina was not at home, she would wait until she returned.

As the Hackney carriage drove off, the door opened and the butler who had let her in the night before greeted her,

"Good morning, Miss Amesly."

"Is Mrs. Bracebridge at home?" Tania asked him.

"She's in the library, miss, and I am sure she'll be right pleased to see you."

Because he spoke so pleasantly, Tania felt some of the agitation inside her chest subside.

She managed to smile at him.

"I would be very grateful if she could see me for a moment please."

"I'm certain that she'd be delighted, miss,"

He did not ask her to wait, but led the way down a passage and opened a door.

"Miss Tania Amesly, ma'am," he announced.

Selina was at the writing desk near the window and she turned round in some surprise and then smiled as Tania came into the room.

"I was not expecting you so soon, Tania."

Then as Tania walked towards her, she exclaimed,

"What has happened? Something has upset you!"

"Oh, please, please, Mrs. Bracebridge help me. I am desperate and I have run away."

"Run away from what, Tania?"

As she saw how agitated Tania was, she suggested,

"Sit down on the sofa, my dear, take off your hat and then tell me what has frightened you."

"That is just the right word. I am frightened, very frightened and did not know what to do, so I came round to you as quickly as I could."

"That's very sensible of you, Tania. Now what can it be? You seemed so happy last night."

"I was happy, very happy except, as I expect you know by now, war has been declared."

"Yes, of course I know. Sir Sidney Herbert told us after everyone had left. I suppose that nice Rupert More is already moving his troops out of Barracks."

"He is going – to the battlefield," Tania murmured.

There was a noticeable break in her voice she could not prevent and Selina enquired,

"Is that what is upsetting you, Tania?"

"No. It's my stepmother."

"What has she done now?"

"She has told me I have to marry a man I met only yesterday. He is called Lord Watford and he apparently desires a young wife."

"Lord Watford! But, of course, you cannot marry him! He has a very bad reputation with women. He was exceedingly unkind to his young wife, which I am certain contributed to her death."

"But Stepmama is determined I am to marry him. He saw me yesterday and he apparently wants someone young who will give him a son."

"I have never heard of such disgraceful behaviour. You cannot marry a man of that age who you don't love."

She hesitated for a moment.

"I don't want to embarrass you, Tania, but I thought last night that perhaps you had fallen in love with Rupert More. He was obviously, I thought, in love with you. Am I right or am I wrong? You must forgive me for asking."

"You are right, *you are right*," cried Tania. "I love Rupert and he loves me, but he did say that because he was going away, he would not tie me down. Therefore I just have to pray that he will come back from the war. Then if God is kind – we can be together for ever."

Selina smiled with delight.

"That is exactly what I hoped would happen, and of course, dear child, you must tell your stepmother that you cannot possibly marry anyone else while Rupert is away."

"But you do not understand. My Stepmama is so determined to be rid of me and according to Papa's will she is my Guardian until I am either twenty-one or married – "

She paused for breath before she went on,

"I am sure it is her idea – that Lord Watford should make me his wife and she said if I do not obey her, she will – have me put into an asylum for women – who are mad."

The last words came jerkily from between her lips.

Selina stared at her in sheer astonishment.

"How could *anyone* say that to you?"

"My stepmother hates me so much – she always has and unless you save me she will do exactly what I have just told you."

Now the tears began to run down Tania's cheeks.

Selina took her handkerchief and wiped them away.

"Don't cry, dearest child. Charles and I will look after you."

"But Stepmama will come and take me away. She is so determined to have what she wants and because she wishes to be rid of me, she will somehow succeed in doing what she said. Oh, why, oh why did Papa marry her?"

"It is something I have often asked myself and so have many others. Your mother was so charming and so sweet. Charles and I loved her as she loved us."

Her voice sharpened as Selina carried on,

"But you are not to worry! I promise you we will not allow your stepmother or a whole Regiment of soldiers to make you marry a man you do not love. As for putting you into an asylum, that is where Isobel Amesly should be herself!

"I must talk to Charles. In the meantime sit quietly here and I will get you something to drink."

She rose as she spoke, then stopped.

"Does your stepmother know where you are?"

"No! She has no idea," answered Tania. "I ran out of the house without her knowing to come to you and there was only one footman in the hall. I did not take a Hackney carriage until I was outside in the road."

"Well, that is one point in our favour – "

Selina walked towards the door.

"Now sit down like a good girl. Don't worry so, Charles and I will save you however difficult it may seem."

Selina's reassuring tone told Tania even more than words that she meant what she said.

She closed her eyes tightly and said a little prayer of thankfulness. She had met the Bracebridges by chance on the ferry and yet they had shown her such kindness.

'I am so lucky to have found them,' she reflected.

She longed to be in touch with Rupert, but knew it would be wrong to do so – whatever happened he must not go off to war being worried about her.

Selina was not away very long and she came back with her husband.

Charles bent down and kissed Tania.

"Selina has told me of the trouble you are in," he said, "and you must not worry. We will look after you and make sure that evil woman does not get hold of you again."

"Are you really sure you can?" Tania asked him.

"Absolutely sure, Tania, and we have both already thought of something you can do to take you a long way away from the clutches of stepmother. And nearer in fact to Rupert More, who I understand now means a great deal to you."

Tania was listening to him intently, but Charles at once realised that she did not understand.

"What my wife has suggested to me," he said, "and I think it is an excellent idea, is that you hide with Florence Nightingale, or rather spend as much time with her as you possibly can. Sidney Herbert told us last night he intends to persuade the Government that she should go out to the war and look after our soldiers *and you could go with her.*"

"You mean she is going as a nurse?" Tania asked in astonishment.

"If Sidney has his way and I am sure he will, she will take very many nurses with her and for the first time in history they will look after the wounded as they should be looked after. She will save them not only from the enemy but from the inefficiency of our doctors who have not had the same training as she has had."

Tania's eyes lit up.

"I would just love to go with Miss Nightingale. It is the most wonderful idea I have ever heard. But do you think she will take me?"

"I think my wife and I will be able to persuade her to do so," Charles answered her. "And what is more, as we are good friends, if she is sent to the war area, as I am sure she will be, we will certainly go with her. So you will be under our care as well as hers."

"*How* can you be so kind?" Tania mumbled as once again the tears ran down her cheeks.

She could hardly believe after being so frightened by her stepmother's threats that she would now be saved and befriended by these two marvellous people.

"Thank – you! Thank you!" she faltered. "I don't know – how to tell you how incredibly grateful – I am."

CHAPTER SIX

It was Charles Bracebridge who sat down to make all the arrangements.

He next turned to his wife,

"Now take Tania off at once to meet Florence and leave everything else to me."

Before he hurried away Tania managed to say,

"I arranged for all the clothes I bought yesterday to be delivered to my home today. So please, please prevent them from going to Amesly House if you possibly can, or my stepmother will be certain to keep them all for herself!"

"I will certainly do my best, Tania. Which shops did they come from?"

Tania gave him the address of the Bond Street shop where she had bought so many clothes as well as the hat shop as she had taken away with her only the hat she was wearing.

She was to learn later that Charles had gone straight to the dress shop and as everything was ready, he took the gowns away in his own carriage and he did the same with the hats.

Then he went to the kitchen door of Amesly House and asked to see Dawson.

He knew him well from the many visits he had paid to Tania's mother and father when they were alive.

Dawson was delighted to see him.

"You be a sight for sore eyes, sir," he said, "and I were so glad to hear you were that kind to Miss Tania on her journey from France."

"I am going to be a great deal kinder to her now," Charles whispered, "because she has run away and I need your help."

Dawson looked over his shoulder to make sure that no one was listening and then stepped outside the kitchen door and closed it behind him.

"The footman tells me that Miss Tania's gone out, sir, but I weren't aware she's no intention of coming back."

"She has very wisely decided to put herself in my and my wife's hands," responded Charles, "but as you will appreciate, she only has what she is wearing and if you can fetch me some clothes from her room, Dawson, without her Ladyship's knowledge, it would be very helpful."

"Leave it to me, sir – "

Charles went to sit in his carriage in the Mews.

Ten minutes later Dawson appeared carrying a case with him.

"I'm only bringing the personal things Miss Tania will need and all the new dresses I understands she bought yesterday," Dawson reported as he reached the carriage.

"It was clever of you to think of that, Dawson, and I see you brought her some flowers as well."

"They was sent to her this morning, and I thinks as they were from the young gentleman she fancies and she'll want them wherever she be."

"You are a genius," exclaimed Charles, tipping him generously. "And if any letters come for Miss Tania let me have them and not her Ladyship."

"You can be sure about that, sir!"

Charles drove away feeling he had done a good job and felt relieved that Lady Amesly was not yet aware that Tania was missing.

When he arrived back at Belgrave Square, it was to find that Selina and Tania had already left for Number One Harley Street.

It then struck him that he should have suggested to them that Tania should now use an assumed name.

Her parents might have known some of the patients who were or had been in the nursing home.

Selina, however, had had the intelligence to realise that if Tania was hiding, there must be no one in the secret except herself and her husband.

She had ordered a carriage from the stables.

Then she turned to Tania,

"We must think of a name for you. I think it would be a mistake even for Florence Nightingale to know who you are."

Tania's eyes widened.

But she realised without arguing about it that Selina was being sensible.

"What shall I call myself?" she asked.

"Have you another name?"

"Yes, I was christened 'Mary Tania'. Mary was my mother's first name and that is why I was called 'Tania'."

"Then I think Mary Anson would be easy for you to remember and it could not be connected in anyone's mind with your stepmother."

"You are so clever!" sighed Tania.

Selina smiled.

"We have to be clever over this and I feel certain that you will want to go out to Turkey with Florence."

Tania gave a cry of delight.

"But of course I want to. I would be near to Rupert even if I cannot see him."

"Then what you must do," suggested Selina, "is to make yourself indispensable to Florence. Thus I intend to tell her that I have been worried about her doing too much herself and it will be even worse if Sidney Herbert has his way. Therefore she definitely needs a secretary."

"You don't think she will consider me too young?" Tania questioned her in a frightened voice.

"You may be rather young, but you have had a very good education, far better than most secretaries have, and I believe quite a number of languages."

"That is true. Having been so long in France my French is perfect, but as well I speak Spanish, German, and a little Greek. So it should not be too difficult for me to learn to speak at least some Turkish."

"Splendid, Tania! Now pray really hard that I can convince Florence that she needs you."

When they arrived at the nursing home, Selina left Tania in the waiting room and went to find Florence.

When she arrived back about twenty minutes later, she was smiling.

"*We have won*," she cried and took Tania to meet Florence Nightingale.

Like everyone else Tania found her an irresistibly attractive woman who was totally different in every way from anyone else she had ever encountered.

From the moment they shook hands she was ready, as many others were to be in the future, to serve Florence and to help her in every possible way.

Tania was allocated a bedroom on the second floor of the nursing home, while Selina went back to bring what luggage Charles had been able to collect for her.

Tania sat down on her bed and said a little prayer of thankfulness.

She was safe from her stepmother.

More important than anything else in the world she would be near Rupert if Florence Nightingale was allowed to go to Turkey.

*

She found that the work she had to do at Number One Harley Street took more time than she expected.

At the same time it was comparatively easy.

Her job initially was to answer the large number of letters Florence received from people asking her advice on their health.

She wrote endless cheques for the tradesmen's bills and kept accounts of everyone who visited or stayed at the nursing home – they might be requesting admittance or had come to discuss their ailments with Florence.

Selina had told Tania it would be a great mistake for her to pop in and out of Belgrave Square.

And she and Charles were very determined to help Florence to go to the war zone.

The first thing they had to do was to assist her in finding nurses to accompany her.

Even before Florence received her invitation from the War Office, she was assured in her mind that this was the work God had chosen for her.

For she had refused marriage and dedicated her life wholly to the purpose of healing and nursing.

It had been very difficult for Sir Sidney Herbert to persuade the Government that she should go to Turkey.

He was supported in his effort by his wife, Liz, who wrote to Lady Stratford de Redcliffe, the wife of the then British Ambassador in Constantinople saying,

"This is not a Lady, but a real hospital nurse and she has had a wealth of experience."

When he finally won his way, Sir Sidney Herbert was delighted.

He had managed to obtain for Florence not only the Government's approval but an official status.

It took time, but in the end he could offer Florence the Official appointment of *Superintendent of the Female Nursing Establishment of the British General Hospital for Turkey*.

It was to be a brave effort besides a difficult one, as no woman had ever been employed as a nurse to wounded soldiers.

As several Members of the Government grumbled,

"Deep prejudice will inevitably be aroused."

However, supported by the Duke of Newcastle, Sir Sidney Herbert secured the agreement of the Cabinet to the appointment.

Florence Nightingale was to be given full authority over the seclusion, disposition and welfare of her nurses.

But they were all to come under the orders of the Chief Medical Officer on the spot, whose name was Doctor Menzies and he was to give her 'every aid in his power and every support in the execution of her arduous duties'.

Directions, she was informed, would come from the British Ambassador, Viscount Stratford de Redcliffe, who would afford her every facility and assurance.

She was also told that the passage and salary for the nurses would be paid by the Treasury and she was given one thousand pounds for expenses and after that she was to rely on the Purser of the Forces at Scutari.

All this naturally was not achieved in a hurry.

There were long discussions and consultations and a considerable amount of disapproval.

However, once permission was obtained, Florence had only to collect her nurses before she left.

This was far more difficult than anyone could have expected and Tania was astonished that there were so few volunteers.

An Office was opened in the Herberts' house at 40 Belgrave Square to receive applications.

"I am afraid that you will have a great many to deal with," Tania advised them. "but if you scribble their names and addresses down I will copy them all out carefully each night and keep them in a book, so that we can get in touch with them at any moment."

To her surprise just a trickle came forward and even then they were mostly women Florence had no wish to take abroad with her.

Actually as Tania confided in private to Selina,

"The nurses are not to be paid enough! They are to receive just fourteen shillings a week with board, lodging and uniform. If their conduct is excellent for three months they will receive sixteen shillings – and if they survive for a year eighteen shillings!"

*

In the meantime Tania was to learn that in June the British Army had landed at Varna in Bulgaria on the West coast of the Black Sea.

By this time she had received quite a large number of letters from Rupert.

But she was aware that he did not yet know she had left home or that she was hiding as a secretary to Florence Nightingale under the assumed name of Mary Anson.

His letters, and he wrote to her as frequently as he

could, were intercepted by Dawson as soon as they arrived and when he had the time, he took them over to Charles in Belgrave Square.

Every day Tania scanned the newspapers for news of the Army, but there was very little news reported.

It was not until September that the news came that the British and the French forces had landed on the Crimea with the object of destroying Sebastopol, the Russian naval arsenal on the Black Sea.

There had been a savage battle on the River Alma on September 20th.

"*It was a glorious but bloody victory,*" one reporter wrote, "*but the casualties were high.*"

"Surely we should be leaving by now. They will be needing us," Tania remarked to Florence.

"I really cannot leave until we are ready," Florence replied. "As you will know, Mary, we do not have enough trained nurses and I refuse to take women who have not the slightest notion what to do and might easily do more harm than good."

Then despatches reaching London from *The Times* correspondent, William Russell, shook the nation.

The aftermath of the Battle of Alma had disclosed how completely inadequate Army organisation had been in practice.

Despite endless official promises there was no plan of any sort to cope with the sick and wounded.

"We must go out and help them," Tania exclaimed desperately.

At last the move she felt had been almost cruelly delayed took place.

It was on a Sunday morning the 21st of October that the party left London Bridge to travel to Boulogne and then on to Paris. They spent one night in Paris before setting off again and four nights in Marseilles.

Florence Nightingale had been given assurances by Sir Sidney Herbert and Doctor Menzies that everything she needed was ready for her in Scutari.

It was at Scutari where the Hospital was established to receive the wounded from the battles in the Crimea.

Florence intended to purchase all the provisions and stores she needed in London and transport them with her.

The faithful Charles and Selina agreed with her and Tania went with them and was surprised at the number of items that Florence was determined to spend her money on.

She received a motley crowd of merchants, shop-keepers and dealers, all of whom were only too willing to supply her with anything she wished to buy.

"They will come in useful," she said firmly to all the questions asked about her puchases.

It was on October 27th when the party boarded *The Vectis.*

It was a horrible ship built for carrying special mail from Marseilles to Malta.

It was infested with huge cockroaches and Florence who was a very bad sailor was prostrate with seasickness.

On the second day out *The Vectis* ran into a severe gale and the Stewards' cabin and the Galley were washed overboard and the guns had to be jettisoned.

In atrociously cold weather, *The Vectis*, '*blustering, storming and shrieking,*' as Florence wrote, sailed up to the Bosporus.

They anchored off Seraglio Point the next day and in pouring rain even the majestic City of Constantinople in the distance looked washed out and unattractive.

On the opposite shore stood the enormous Barrack Hospital and it looked extremely gloomy to Tania.

One of the nurses in the party suggested,

"Oh, Miss Nightingale, when we finally land don't let there be any delay by red tape. Let's get straight into nursing those poor fellows."

Florence, however, as she gazed at the gigantic pile, replied quietly,

"The strongest will be wanted at the washtub – "

The Vectis anchored at breakfast time.

Lord Stratford de Redcliffe had sent Lord Napier, the Secretary of the Embassy, to welcome them.

He was very polite and told Florence that it would give him great happiness to serve her.

He also suggested that the nurses should go to the Hospital at once as many wounded men had arrived from a battle at Balaclava that had been fought more than a week earlier – and a great many more were expected.

Several caiques, the local gondola-like boats of the Bosporus, appeared and the nurses were lowered into them with their carpetbags and umbrellas.

Then the party was rowed across to Scutari.

Tania with Charles and Selina by her, looked across at the huge ugly square building with a tower at its centre.

It dominated the scruffy little village of Scutari and it had been a Turkish Army Barracks and now it was the Barrack Hospital where they were to start work with the wounded.

Tania could only hope that it was better inside than it appeared from the outside.

Her wish was not granted.

The state of the Barrack Hospital was much worse than even Florence Nightingale had anticipated.

They were soon to find out that there was enormous prejudice against a woman bursting in on what was always considered a man's affair – especially when they were to find a shocking state of inefficiency and neglect.

The rain had ceased by the time the last caique had rowed across the Bosporus, but there was mud everywhere and Tania saw the bloated carcase of a horse that had been washed up on the shore and was being worried by a pack of starving dogs.

They made their way over to the gate of the great building behind the nurses.

Doctor Menzies, the Medical Officer in charge, and Major Sillery, the Military Commandant, were waiting to receive them.

Florence was quick over the conversation that took place on their arrival asking brusquely to see their quarters.

One room only had been allocated to the fourteen Hospital nurses.

There was a tiny room ten feet square for Florence which she decided to share with Selina.

There was another which she said would have to be a sitting room, an Office and Charles's bedroom.

It was obvious that there was no place for Tania.

A room on the first floor was taken by ten nurses, but only after the body of a dead Russian General had been moved out.

"Where am I to sleep?" Tania asked desperately.

Finally they found exactly opposite the sitting room and Office that there was a large cupboard with a number of shelves that had been intended for laundry.

Fortunately it contained a minute window that had obviously not been opened in many years and when pushed by Charles's strong hands it let in damp air.

There was just room on the floor for a bed after the bottom shelves were removed and Tania realised that she would have to lift all she required down from overhead.

At least, she told herself, she would be alone and not have to share with any of the other women whom she found rather uncongenial.

In the whole Hospital there were no tables, not even one for operations.

There was nothing at all to cook with, and the daily allowance of water for all purposes was fixed at one pint per person.

When the doctors left them, Florence exploded,

"This place is filthy, dilapidated and verminous!"

They were to find that the wards for the wounded soldiers were far worse than their own accommodation.

The filth and smell was beyond description.

The woodwork was rotten, so that it could not be scrubbed, and saturated with filth it became a paradise for germs and vermin.

There were scarcely any blankets and the soldiers lay in their dirty shirts which they refused to part with – if they did, they were given another dirty shirt with a dead man's lice in it.

Six hundred hospital dresses had been sent before they left England, so Florence had been told, but they were never seen again.

Florence found out as soon as they arrived that the doctors had no intention of allowing her to have anything to do with the sick and wounded.

She did not make a scene or point out that so many men who were suffering from dysentery and cholera were dying unattended.

Obeying her orders that the nurses were not to go near the wounded men, she started to clean up the Hospital.

Florence herself stood over the tubs and helped to scrub in a forlorn attempt to reduce infections.

A number of sick and wounded men were brought to the Hospital every day from the battlefield on the other side of the Black Sea.

Men who had suffered acutely for days in the slow and ill-equipped ships bringing them from the Crimea were dying before they could be carried into the Hospital. After rolling about on the open decks without drugs, dressings or even blankets, many were taken straight to the graveyard.

Ignored by the doctors, Florence soon realised that she was to be frozen out as not one doctor would use her nurses or her supplies.

Although the men were in desperate need and she could give them all that was required from her purchases in London, her stores were refused.

According to Army regulations, Hospital orderlies were the only assistants to be used by the doctors and they were usually weak, stupid and clumsy – and as the work of tending the sick was forced on them they naturally disliked it and did as little as possible.

Florence was clever enough to realise that before she could achieve anything she had to win the confidence of the doctors.

She was determined not to offer her nurses or her stores again, but to wait until the doctors asked for help.

It was a policy that demanded huge self-control and she had to stand back, see men suffer and do nothing until officially instructed.

Several days passed and more stores did arrive.

Florence made her nurses sort out the old linen and count packages of provisions.

The endless cries of men in pain were unanswered while the nurses did not dare to go to them.

They all criticised Florence, but she remained silent and some of the nurses formed the impression that she was indifferent to the suffering of the wounded.

One thing Florence did note as soon as she arrived was that the Hospital food was virtually inedible even for healthy men and as a diet for cholera and dysentery cases it produced agony.

On the very day she had arrived, Florence began to cook. She had brought arrowroot, wine and beer and other potable stores in Marseilles.

She provided pails of hot arrowroot and port wine for those who needed it and within only a week the kitchen belonging to her quarters had become an extra diet kitchen for the Hospital.

Food was cooked under the direction of two nurses and Tania, who had learned to cook at her school in France was particularly good at it.

This kitchen was the only means of supplying food in the whole Hospital, but still no nurse was permitted to give a patient any nourishment without a doctor's written consent.

Then on November 9th ships bringing the wounded from the battle of Inkerman, fought four days before, began to arrive and unload at Scutari.

The men had suffered frightfully on the journey and several soldiers died before they even reached the Hospital.

The situation now completely changed as a flood of sick and wounded men poured into Scutari on such a scale that a crisis of urgency arose and prejudice against nursing women was forgotten for the moment.

Tania now helped the nurses in the wards as if she was one of them.

She had found herself attending to the wounded leg of a young corporal who she realised from what remained of his uniform was a Grenadier.

This she knew was Rupert's Regiment in the First Division.

"That be better, missie," he sighed after Tania had washed his leg thoroughly and put bandages over a healing cream supplied by Florence.

"You are not really very seriously wounded," Tania said with a smile. "But it must have been a terrible battle."

"That it were," he replied. "Yet I thinks us won it."

Then somewhat tentatively she asked him,

"Did you happen by any chance see Captain Rupert More – before or during the battle?"

"I sees him right enough," the corporal answered, "and he were ridin' a fine horse. But when he then gallops against them Russian guns, I sees the Captain fall."

Tania drew in her breath horrified.

Then she managed to ask in a voice which did not sound like her own,

"*Do you mean he was killed*?"

"No. I thinks it be his horse them Ruskies got, not him. I did see him fall, but he must have been wounded, 'cos they carries him away afore they takes me down the hill and puts me on the ship as brings me here."

"Where was he taken?" Tania demanded.

"To a big yacht that were in the harbour."

Tania gathered up her bandages and cream.

Then because she could not help herself she ran out of the ward to look for Selina.

She was cutting up bandages in the small Office in which her husband slept and Charles was sitting near the window reading a newspaper.

Tania rushed into the room.

"I have just heard from one of the wounded men," she cried breathlessly, "that Rupert has been wounded. He is not dead, but has been taken to a yacht in the harbour."

Selina stared at her and then she gasped,

"I think Rupert must be on Lord Cardigan's yacht. A doctor told me that everyone was talking about it."

"You think that perhaps Rupert is a friend of Lord Cardigan?" asked Tania.

Charles turned round and commented,

"I suppose what you are really saying is that you want to go and see him, Tania?"

"Oh, please, please, if it is possible for me to do so. You cannot imagine how frightened I have been ever since all these men arrived from Inkerman. If Rupert is wounded I must see him – just in case – "

Her voice failed and she could not say the words.

Charles and Selina knew that she was thinking,

' – he dies.'

"Leave it to me," Charles offered. "In the meantime go on with your good work. You know that Florence has been waiting for this moment and we must now prove how cruel and idiotic those doctors have been in keeping her out of the wards until now."

"I know – but please promise me you will try to see if anyone can take me to – Lord Cardigan's yacht."

Despite her every effort the tears ran down her face as she spoke.

Charles recognised just how much she must have suffered in keeping silent for so long.

He and Selina had very deliberately not mentioned Rupert, just in case they were making a mistake and there was no real feeling between them.

Now they were convinced without being told that Tania was very much in love with him.

Selina hurried out of the room with her bandages and Charles could only hope that if Tania did go to visit Rupert, he would not, like so many men who had fought at Inkerman, be dead or dying.

Tania did not go back to the ward where she had been working.

Instead she went to find Florence.

It was now late and she thought it was too dark to see very clearly.

There were four miles of corridors in the hospital and with the new wounded soldiers arriving, every corridor was crammed with patients lying on stuffed sacks and there was only just enough room to pass between them.

Every single night, even when Florence herself had not been permitted to do anything for the wounded, Tania had gone the rounds.

She spoke to the patients and gave them at least some idea that someone cared.

To light her way in the wards she carried a Turkish lantern of a single candle inside a circular shade.

It was this, although neither Florence nor Tania had any idea of it then, that was to give Florence the name of '*The Lady with the Lamp*'.

She inspired the historic poem that was written later by Longfellow,

"*Lo! In that hour of misery*
A Lady with a lamp I see
Pass through the glimmering gloom,
And flit from room to room.
And slow, as in a dream of bliss,

The speechless sufferer turns to kiss

Her shadow, as it falls

Upon the darkening walls."

After Tania had left, Charles went to call on Lord Stratford de Redcliffe, who was virtually a dictator and the Turks called him 'The Great Elchi', the Great Ambassador.

Physically he was extremely handsome and prided himself on his looks.

He lived in a magnificent Palace in Constantinople and travelled with twenty-five servants and seven tons of plate.

Unfortunately he had done little to help the Barrack Hospital and Florence had somewhat unkindly described him as 'bad-tempered, heartless, pompous and lazy'.

He enjoyed associating with Kings and Emperors, he was jealous of his inferiors and was certainly not a man to interest himself in a hospital for common soldiers.

'*For two years,*' Florence wrote, '*he has had the British Army perishing within sight of his window and has done nothing about it.*'

At the same time Charles knew that Lord Stratford was the one person who could make it possible for Tania to visit Rupert.

He reckoned with a sarcastic smile that as Rupert came from a most distinguished family and his father was an Earl, Lord Stratford would be pleased to oblige!

CHAPTER SEVEN

When Charles called in at Lord Stratford's opulent Palace, he gave his name and said that his business with his Lordship was 'important and urgent'.

He was, however, somewhat surprised when a few minutes later he was escorted into a large beautiful room overlooking the Bosporus.

Lord Stratford who was reading a newspaper put it on one side, stood up and shook hands.

"I am delighted to see you, Mr. Bracebridge, and I do apologise for not calling on you when you first arrived. But I know you have been very busy and so indeed have I."

"I have come to see you, my Lord, on an errand of mercy," replied Charles, "but first I must tell you a secret that is known to no one else since we left England."

He saw Lord Stratford was intrigued and he then sat down and told him who Tania was.

And why they had brought her away on this most difficult assignment with Florence Nightingale.

Lord Stratford listened to him without speaking and then he exclaimed,

"I have never heard anything so appalling as Lady Amesly's behaviour. Of course you were right to bring the poor girl away with you."

"She had already lost her heart before we left home to Captain Rupert More," Charles went on. "I expect you know he is a son of the Earl of Grantmore and we have just learnt that he has been wounded at Inkerman."

"He is sadly one of many. You may not know that he has just lost his elder brother."

Charles looked at him in surprise.

"His brother! Do you mean Viscount Grant?"

"I was reading in the English newspapers just two days ago, which take more than a week coming here, that Viscount Grant has died in India of a rare fever that none of the doctors could cure."

"I had no idea!" exclaimed Charles. "Our English newspapers have not arrived now for nearly ten days."

"It was explained at some length that the Viscount who has been an Equerry to the Governor, would be a great loss to India and naturally to his father the Earl."

"This will mean," said Charles slowly, "that Rupert More now takes on his brother's title. You will understand, my Lord, that Tania Amesly, who knows nothing of what you have just told me, is most anxious to be with him."

"Of course I understand, and I will give you every possible assistance. Have you any idea where he is?"

"The young soldier Tania was treating this morning had just come from Inkerman. He said that he saw Rupert being carried onto a yacht. I gather the only private yacht in Balaclava Harbour belongs to Lord Cardigan."

"Indeed that is where Cardigan is! I must make it my business to call on him, which I have not done for the simple reason that they were anticipating a violent battle."

There was a pause in the conversation.

"I tell you what I'll do," suggested Lord Stratford. "I will lend you my yacht early tomorrow morning to take you and Miss Amesly to Balaclava Harbour."

"That is exceedingly kind of you, my Lord, and I cannot tell you how grateful I am."

"I am quite certain that if the wounded Rupert is at present with Lord Cardigan, he will be only too pleased to accommodate Miss Amesly, and then you can return in my yacht."

"I will be waiting for it at eight o'clock," Charles said, "and thank you, my Lord, for your great kindness and understanding, which I deeply appreciate."

Lord Stratford offered him some refreshment, but Charles said it would be a mistake to waste any more time. So he thanked him again and returned to the Hospital.

Tania was waiting for him.

As he stepped out of the caique that had rowed him from Lord Stratford's Palace, she ran down to the water's edge and threw herself against him.

"What did he say? *Will he help me*?"

"Everything is arranged, Tania, and we are to leave at eight o'clock tomorrow morning. I am going to take you to Lord Cardigan's yacht in Balaclava Harbour."

"Oh, you are wonderful! *Wonderful*!" cried Tania.

*

She slept very little that night and started dressing before six o'clock.

She put on one of the pretty dresses she had bought in London and then she packed her clothes, saying a prayer as she did so that she would not be sent away before she had seen Rupert.

Later Selina came and helped her as Tania was still putting her last things into boxes on the floor outside the cupboard she slept in.

"I do hope Lord Cardigan will let you stay with

Rupert," said Selina. "But if you have to come back here, you know Charles and I will be very happy to look after you."

"I am only afraid they may refuse to let me go on Lord Cardigan's yacht and Rupert might be too ill to see me."

"I am sure you will see him and you will be able to find out if the letters you wrote ever reached him."

"I am sure the letters I wrote to him from here did not. Otherwise he would have replied to me."

That morning Tania had breakfast at seven o'clock with Selina and later Charles joined them.

"I think that the earlier we set off for Balaclava the better," he said. "I can see ships heading in this direction which means that more wounded are likely to arrive at any moment. I had better get Tania away before she is given a dozen things to do that would delay our departure."

Tania kissed Selina.

"I think it is a bit over-optimistic of me to take my clothes with me. Lord Cardigan may not have me to stay."

She drew in her breath before she added,

"At the same time if Rupert is to be sent home as he is wounded, I am determined to go with him."

"Of course you must," agreed Selina, "and as you have been taught by Florence what to do, no one else will be able to look after him as well as you could."

"I hope you are right," sighed Tania, "but they may make it very difficult for me."

Selina realised that she was referring to the doctors and she thought it best not to discuss any of the difficulties.

It was not until they were aboard the elegant yacht owned by Lord Stratford that Charles told Tania what he had learnt about Rupert's brother.

"I never thought, as he was in India, that he would be in danger," commented Tania. "Actually Rupert did not say very much about him at all."

"I am not surprised. I understand the two brothers did not get on and the late Viscount was not a popular man in London."

"He didn't see eye to eye with his father either, who had no wish for him to go to India with their large estate in the country to manage. He thought that one son as a soldier was more than enough."

Tania did not say anything as she was thinking with a sudden fear she could not describe that if Rupert died too the Earl would be childless.

Lord Stratford's yacht was waiting just below them and it was fortunate there was no other ship unloading the wounded at that moment.

Charles made one of the orderlies carry her cases down to the yacht and then he kissed his wife goodbye and Tania did the same.

"Thank you, thank you for all you have done for me," she said to Charles and Selina, "you have been so wonderful and please do explain to Miss Nightingale how grateful I am to her. I will not say goodbye to her because she might be supervising a delicate operation and praying that the suffering soldier will survive."

"You are right, my dear," sighed Selina. "Florence would hate you to interfere at such a time, but I will tell her what you have said."

Tania kissed Selina goodbye again and then hurried down to Charles who was already boarding the yacht.

*

It took them two days to cross the Black Sea and reach Balaclava Harbour.

There were two ships in the port waiting to convey more wounded from the Battle of Inkerman to the Hospital and *The Dryad*, Lord Cardigan's yacht, looked, because it was so smart and elegant, completely out of place.

Many felt that it was a fairytale vessel. It had been sailed from England, Tania was to discover later, by Lord Cardigan's French chef.

Lord Cardigan himself lived a life of luxury on his yacht while his men suffered endless privations in tents on the cold and windy Russian plain.

The Cavalry he commanded were stationed several miles from the Harbour and the Regimental Brigadier was obliged to come to the yacht every evening to receive his orders for the next day.

By what had seemed a miracle Lord Cardigan had survived unscathed when he had ridden with the Charge of the Light Brigade.

His Cavalrymen endured what was described as the most appalling slaughter of riders and horses ever seen in the history of warfare.

Five hundred horses of the Light Brigade were lost, and the Seventeenth Lancers were very nearly completely annihilated.

When they reached the Harbour, it was possible for Lord Stratford's yacht to come alongside *The Dryad*.

Charles climbed out first and as he did so he was aware that Tania was tense with anxiety.

She had hardly spoken a word as they crossed the Black Sea and he realised just how much she was suffering waiting to learn if Rupert was still alive or how badly he might be wounded.

She was trembling as they walked up the gangway of *The Dryad*.

There was a sentry standing on the deck.

"Is his Lordship aboard?" Charles asked him.

"He's just returned, sir," the man answered.

"Would you be good enough to inform his Lordship that Mr. Charles Bracebridge wishes to see him – "

"Will you come this way, sir."

The sentry led the way to the Saloon.

There was no one in it and it was, as Tania saw, an exceedingly comfortable and elegant room.

Both she and Charles were silent as they waited and then they heard a voice just outside the door.

A moment later Lord Cardigan walked in.

He was even better looking than had been reported with a most charming smile that even his detractors found difficult to resist.

"I am delighted to meet you, Mr. Bracebridge," he began. "I heard that you and your wife had accompanied Miss Florence Nightingale out to Scutari, and I thought it extremely brave of you."

"We brought with us Miss Tania Amesly, my Lord. Her father, Lord Amesly, you may have known."

"Of course I have met him in the House of Lords," Lord Cardigan replied, turning to Tania and holding out his hand, "but I had no idea he had such a beautiful daughter."

"We are here, my Lord," Charles went on, "having heard, although we may have been misinformed, that you have very kindly taken onboard Captain Rupert More who has been seriously wounded."

"That's true. I have known him since he was a child and I could not allow him to suffer lying wounded in a cold tent."

"That is so good of you, my Lord," Tania came in.

"He is in a weak condition, but the wound was not as severe as was at first thought."

"*Then Rupert is – alive*?" Tania mumbled in a voice he could hardly hear.

"Yes, he is most definitely alive, Miss Amesly, and I expect that you would like to see him."

"That is why I have come here, my Lord, and if it is possible I would like to nurse him."

Lord Cardigan looked a bit surprised and raised his eyebrows, but he did not say what he was thinking.

Instead he suggested,

"Let me take you down to Rupert's cabin and you will see for yourself that with good nursing and a sensible diet he will soon, we hope, be himself again."

There was no need for him to guess just how much Tania wanted to see Rupert.

He could see it in her face and the sudden light in her eyes.

Lord Cardigan smiled at Tania.

"Do come with me. I think it would be wise if Mr. Bracebridge stays on here, so that there are not too many people in the cabin at the same time.

"I will wait, my Lord," Charles agreed.

Lord Cardigan led the way below.

As he did so, Tania was aware that the yacht was even bigger than she had expected it to be.

And this made her hope, although she could not put it into words, that he would allow her to stay on board and nurse Rupert back to health.

Lord Cardigan opened the door of a cabin and she saw that it was quite a large one.

Rupert was lying face upward with his eyes closed on a comfortable berth draped with muslin curtains.

As Tania moved towards him, she could see that his left shoulder was heavily bandaged.

Neither she nor Lord Cardigan spoke.

Then Rupert opened his eyes.

As he saw Tania his whole face, which had seemed so pale and lifeless, suddenly changed completely –

"Tania!" he cried. "*Am I dreaming*? I have died and gone to Heaven!"

Tania ran forward and knelt down beside him.

"I am here, Rupert! I heard you had been wounded and I came as quickly as I could."

"My darling, my sweet! But how is it possible you are here and in this Godforsaken part of the world?"

"I have written to you each and every day, Rupert, but my letters never reached you. I came here with those wonderful angels, Selina and Charles Bracebridge, who are with Florence Nightingale."

"I thought they would be, but I had no idea that you would come with them, Tania."

"I am here and I want to nurse you – and make you well again."

"I am so much better already simply because you are near me, my darling."

Lord Cardigan without saying anything, walked to the door and going out of the cabin closed it behind him.

Then he went back to the Saloon.

"I think," he said to Charles, "we have found the one medicine that will make Rupert well more quickly than anything the doctors can prescribe!"

"He was well enough to recognise her, my Lord?"

"Very much so and now I think it's time for a glass of champagne. That is certainly something I need myself after just coming from the Battlefield of Inkerman."

"I understand the death toll was exceedingly high?"

"Terrible, terrible."

They drank their champagne and then talked of the inadequacy of the High Command.

History was going to prove that the Charge of the Light Brigade nearly three weeks ago was a fine example of what courage, determination and discipline will achieve however misguided.

After he had conversed with Charles for some time, Lord Cardigan enquired,

"Now tell me what I am expected to do about this beautiful young woman you have brought aboard."

Charles told him, just as he had told Lord Stratford, why Tania had come to him and his wife for help.

Lord Cardigan was astonished.

"I have never heard of such a thing," he blustered. "I have met the second Lady Amesly and I always thought her a pushy and unpleasant woman despite her good looks. But I could never imagine her doing anything so appalling to her stepdaughter!"

"Fortunately, my Lord, we managed to spirit Tania away, otherwise her stepmother, being her Guardian, could have forced her to marry Lord Watford and there is nothing we could have possibly done to prevent it."

"I understand, Mr. Bracebridge, and I believe it is an appalling law which should be repealed."

Charles smiled.

"That is up to you in the House of Lords."

"If I return – it is a miracle I was not killed as so many of my wretched men were. And between ourselves we think that the Russians are planning a second attack at

Inkerman that may cost us just as much to repulse as their previous attack."

"If only our Army was bigger," Charles murmured.

"I agree with you, but at least one man will survive, and I think if it is at all possible he should go home."

"Rupert – back to England?" asked Charles with a note of surprise in his voice.

"Why not? He will not be fit to fight again for at least a year and in my humble opinion the sooner that we get the wounded out of the way the better."

"I agree with you," replied Charles. "But how will he travel? That could be a problem."

"As far as Rupert is concerned, and because I have always been very fond of him, I should think the best way would be for him to travel home by sea."

"I agree with you, my Lord."

Charles was thinking of how the wounded had been conveyed from the battlefield to the Hospital, lying on the decks of ships, being rolled about and splashed by waves.

"If Rupert could find a small yacht, not as large as mine, of course – and I believe they are obtainable locally – he and his pretty lady friend could travel back in comfort. I would not mind betting that he would be almost fit again by the time they reach England."

"It is certainly an idea, my Lord."

"And I am quite certain that the expense of renting a yacht would not be a problem to his father, who will of course want him home."

Then Charles remembered what Lord Stratford had told him and said,

"I don't know if you have been told, my Lord, that Rupert's elder brother, Viscount Grant, has died in India. Lord Stratford told me about it before I came here to you."

"Then that makes it even more essential for him to survive. I most certainly would be prepared to order his return to England if it is possible to find a way for him to be conveyed there."

"In the meanwhile, my Lord, are you prepared to have Tania as a guest and nurse on your yacht?"

"I would be delighted, Mr. Bracebridge. I am only sorry that anyone so beautiful will, as far as I can see, not be aware I even exist."

Both men laughed and Charles added,

"I will now go and find, as you have suggested, a yacht which Rupert can buy, to convey two happy young people back to the country so many have just died for."

Lord Cardigan gave a deep sigh.

"I am only praying that the mistakes we have made already will not be repeated in the future."

"And I say 'amen' to that, my Lord."

Tania's luggage was collected from the yacht.

Only when he had sent it aboard *The Dryad* and seen it placed in a cabin next door to Rupert's did Charles quietly open his cabin door.

Tania was sitting by the bed and her hand was in Rupert's.

But Charles saw that for the moment his eyes were closed and he was sleeping from sheer exhaustion.

Gently Tania took away her hand and tiptoed across the cabin and when she was outside, Charles shut the door and whispered,

"Lord Cardigan is prepared for you to stay and I have put your luggage in the next cabin. Now I am going, at his suggestion, to try to buy a yacht to convey you and Rupert back to England."

"A yacht!"

"With careful nursing he will in time be completely well and strong enough to make you very happy, Tania, but there is no doubt that his life as a soldier is finished."

"I can only thank God for that. I have learnt that he was shot in the left shoulder and the bullet just touched his lung. He will find it hard to breathe for a time."

Charles made a sympathetic sound.

"I know, because I have seen other men in the same condition," continued Tania, "that he will never be able to run very fast again. Otherwise he will be able to enjoy life as he has always done."

"That is all we need to know – and of course you must be most grateful to Lord Cardigan for accepting you and for making this most useful suggestion."

Tania put her arms round Charles's neck and kissed his cheek.

"You have been wonderful, wonderful to me," she sighed, "and I can never thank you enough."

"I will come back as soon as I have some news."

Tania kissed him again, but did not suggest that she would see him off.

Instead she returned to Rupert's cabin to find him still asleep.

Charles went above to find Lord Cardigan.

He was in the Saloon giving his orders to an Officer who had just arrived and when Charles appeared he walked out onto the deck with him.

"I have been thinking over my advice to you," he said, "and I think if the two young people really love each other, it would be wise for them to be married before they set off for England."

Charles looked at him in surprise.

"Only you, my Lord, would think of a wedding at such a time as this. And only you would be sleeping and working in the most beautiful yacht I have ever seen."

"It is engendering a great deal of envy, hatred and malice here, but I feel I am a better Commander because I am not sleeping in mud and discomfort which affects a man's brain as well as his body."

"I think you are very brave in more ways than one, my Lord."

*

It took Charles over two weeks to find the yacht he wanted.

It was, when finally he had found and bought it, an extremely smart vessel with all modern conveniences and it had been built for a rich Greek, who had by a twist of fate gone bankrupt before he could pay for it.

Because the builder was so out of pocket, the price of the yacht was cheaper than it might have been because there was no prospect of another purchaser.

Charles realised he had secured a bargain and when he brought the yacht into Balaclava Harbour it was greatly admired.

He thought Tania was looking even more beautiful and radiant than he had ever seen her.

"I know you are happy," he remarked, "before you tell me so."

"Of course I am happy, because I am looking after Rupert – and he is happy too because every day his wound is steadily healing."

She paused for a moment before she whispered,

"If he had been treated as those poor soldiers before Florence arrived, he would undoubtedly have died."

"But he is alive, Tania, and I have brought you a yacht to take you both back to England."

"I am glad not just for Rupert's sake. He has heard from his father who is hugely upset over the death of his elder son."

"I was very afraid that he would be, even though I understand they did not get on well together."

"It will mean much more responsibility for Rupert than he has ever had to shoulder before."

"I am sure that whatever he has to do he will do very well, just as I have learnt from Lord Cardigan that he was in every way an excellent soldier."

Charles hesitated before adding,

"And I am sure that you will find him an excellent husband!"

Tania gave a little cry.

"Rupert wants to marry me and I want to marry him more than anything in the whole world. I love him and he loves me and together we can face whatever the future may hold for us."

"Of course you can, Tania."

She gave him messages of thanks and appreciation for Selina and for Florence Nightingale.

She waved Charles affectionately goodbye and then she went back to Rupert.

"Charles Bracebridge has been brilliant – and found us a yacht," she said breathlessly as she entered his cabin.

"You must go and look at it and make sure that it contains everything you want, my darling."

"You know I only want to be with you, Rupert."

Tania sat down beside him and with his good right hand he picked up hers and drew it to his lips.

"I love you. I adore you, my Tania, and did you tell Mr. Bracebridge that we are to be married tonight?"

Tania shook her head.

"I did not tell him because I really should ask him and Selina to be present. But I want to be alone with you as it is going to be a wonderful marvellous service that will carry us up to Heaven itself. I thought that no guest could ever feel what we will feel."

"We have to have a witness and Lord Cardigan has promised to do it for us."

"He will understand what I feel – and I want you to feel it too, Rupert."

She was not mistaken.

The Army Chaplain, who Lord Cardigan had asked to marry them, was a Priest dedicated to the work of God.

He had left a comfortable living in England because he believed that it was his duty to succour the men facing death in the Crimea.

Lord Cardigan, in one of his gestures that made him so popular, had filled Rupert's cabin in the new yacht with white flowers.

Tania put on a dress she had brought with her from London – it was not white, but the pale pink of the sun in the early morning.

It made her look as if she had floated down from the sky and she made a little wreath of white flowers.

Although she wore no veil, Rupert thought that no bride could look lovelier and he knew that he was the most fortunate man alive.

So many of the men who had served with him were dead or had been wounded so severely they would be left crippled for the rest of their lives.

When the doctor had seen him this morning he had said that Tania's bandaging was perfection and he had no criticism to make about it.

Tania knew she had only followed instructions and she had watched closely the way Florence Nightingale had attended to the suffering men in the Scutari Hospital.

She did not even tell Rupert that she prayed while she treated him – and at night and at so many other times.

She believed that in answer to her prayers invisible healing came down from the skies.

His body responded to her as did his spirit.

'I love him! I do love him!' she told herself as she dressed for their quiet wedding.

Then as she left her cabin she was very touched as Lord Cardigan gave her a bouquet that matched the flowers in her hair.

The Marriage Service was simple and short.

Yet the sincerity of the vows of love exchanged between the two of them seemed to make the whole cabin holy.

When the Chaplain blessed them, Tania felt that her mother and father were with her and were happy because she had found the same wonderful love they too had found.

A love she knew could only come from God.

After the Blessing the Chaplain left them together holding hands.

*

When it was nearly dark, Rupert was carried very carefully by Lord Cardigan's men from *The Dryad* to *The Sea Horse*, the yacht that Charles had bought for them.

He had told Rupert that he and Selina would give them the yacht as a wedding present, but Rupert refused.

"It is overwhelmingly generous of you, but I cannot start my married life by being so beholden to two people who have been so marvellous and generous to Tania.

"You hid her from her stepmother and brought her out here to me. You could not have given me anything I wanted more if you had thrown in the sun, the sky and the stars!"

Charles smiled.

"Very well, I will share it with you and you can pay me back half the cost when you reach England. My wife and I will find something we can give you for your home."

"For the moment we will stay at our family house in Park Lane as my father has gone to the country.

"But we will have to spend a great deal of time with him there, not just because it will make him feel happy, but I will now have to look after the estate and our racehorses."

Charles laughed.

"I can see I will not have to worry about you in the future. And now she is your wife I need no longer worry about Tania.

"Actually now that Tania is leaving I do think it is time I took Selina home. We have helped Florence to get started as much as we can and we will be waiting to help her again when she returns to England. But I too have my responsibilities and I have had enough of Scutari Hospital to last me for a lifetime."

"Tania has been telling me all about its horrors and I think you have been absolutely fantastic in staying here so long. No one could have done more for Florence."

"I think that you will find when she does return to England that what she has achieved is not just for England, but suffering men and women all over the world will award her a halo."

"You can be sure of that," agreed Rupert.

Once he had been settled comfortably in the Master Cabin of *The Sea Horse*, Tania bade her farewells to Lord Cardigan and he kissed her.

"Take good care of Rupert, Tania," he urged her, "and he is very special to me and to so many others in his Regiment. I sense that you have a *healing hand* just like Miss Nightingale and, as I can tell that you and Rupert are deeply in love, I imagine that your healing powers will be doubly effective on him."

Lord Cardigan kissed her again.

As soon as he left the yacht, *The Sea Horse* moved slowly out of Balaclava Harbour.

Their Captain had been instructed to take them very leisurely and to avoid rough seas as much as possible.

Tania undressed and went up onto the deck in her dressing gown before she went to bed.

She thought that Rupert had been asleep when she had left him and she stood still for a moment gazing at the moon turning the sea to silver and the stars shining brightly above.

It was difficult to think that it was only so near at hand that men were still dying to further the ambitions and politics of their rulers.

She wanted to pray for peace in the future.

But she knew that it was hopeless to ask for peace when there were still so many ambitious and unscrupulous men in the world.

Instead she prayed, as she had prayed so often, for Rupert's and her happiness and because they had been so fortunate they must bring love and happiness to others.

She went below to find that Rupert was awake.

"I want you, Tania," he sighed. "I thought you had left me."

"Only to look at the moon and to thank God that we are married and that I now belong to you."

"Come close to me," he asked her.

Tania hesitated.

"Suppose I hurt your shoulder?"

"You will not do so if you lie on my right side. I want you near me. I want to feel that now the ring is on your finger, I can never lose you and you are truly mine."

She took off her dressing gown and slipped gently and carefully into the bed beside him.

He put his right arm round her and when he felt the softness of her body against his, he sighed,

"This is all I have ever wanted, Tania. Now I know, my precious beautiful darling, that we are really one."

"I love you. I adore you," she whispered, "and we will never lose each other."

"First I want to get well so I can tell you better that I can tell you now how much you mean to me."

Tania understood what he was saying to her and she put her cheek against his shoulder.

"I am all yours," she murmured. "Utterly yours and nothing in the world could be more perfect than that we are husband and wife sailing towards England. I never want to see this part of the world again, but I will always remember it."

"We will remember it together because you came to me when I desperately needed you, but was terrified that I would lose you."

"You could never have done that, no matter how long you were away, my darling Rupert. This is perfection – this is Heaven."

"Just a small part of it and now, my precious, as I cannot bend over you and kiss you – you must kiss me."

Very gently for fear she might hurt him, she did as he asked.

Her lips met his.

His very touch made her whole body quiver with the ecstasy and wonder of his kiss.

She knew that together they had found the perfect love which would be theirs for ever.

Even when they died they would still reach out and find each other again.

Their love came only from God and would endure for Eternity, for ever and beyond.